SKADI

STEVEN GRIER WILLIAMS

MILFORD
HOUSE

an imprint of Sunbury Press, Inc.
Mechanicsburg, PA USA

MILFORD HOUSE

an imprint of Sunbury Press, Inc.
Mechanicsburg, PA USA

For information about special discounts for bulk purchases, please contact Sunbury Press Orders Dept. at (855) 338-8359 or orders@sunburypress.com.

To request one of our authors for speaking engagements or book signings, please contact Sunbury Press Publicity Dept. at publicity@sunburypress.com.

FIRST MILFORD HOUSE PRESS EDITION: August 2021

Set in Adobe Garamond | Interior design by Crystal Devine | Cover by Derek Thornton | Edited by Abigail Henson.

Publisher's Cataloging-in-Publication Data
Names: Williams, Steven Grier, author.
Title: Skadi / Steven Grier Williams.
Description: First trade paperback edition. | Mechanicsburg, PA : Milford House Press, 2021.
Summary: Children in the town of Fensalir are dying at the hands of a centuries-old jötunn, but a witch named Frija has a plan. She recruits Skadi, a skilled warrior, to venture into Midgard to obtain the power of the World Tree. But Skadi, and Skadi's young son must confront violent Norse mythological creatures in order to return home and save the children.
Identifiers: ISBN : 978-1-62006-637-9 (softcover).
Subjects: Fantasy | FICTION / Fantasy / Action & Adventure | FICTION / Fairy Tales, Folk Tales, Legends & Mythology.

Product of the United States of America
0 1 1 2 3 5 8 13 21 34 55

Continue the Enlightenment!

This book is dedicated to the smartest and strongest women I know: my wife, Danielle Lauren Lisa Williams; my mom, Sharon Hunter Williams; and my sister, Danielle Hunter Williams.

ACKNOWLEDGMENTS

I would like to thank everyone who has taken the time to read my novel, provide feedback, and support my writing over the years. That sort of love has helped me refine my craft.

PROLOGUE

"I think I may have found a champion."

"Is that so?"

"What do you think?"

"I think this won't go as you hope it will."

"There is good that will come of it."

"I know."

"You advised him. You can advise me."

"My advisory always came with a price."

"The path this person is on will help you too."

"It's not a bad plan but be careful. You will be provoking the trickster."

ONE

WINTER

Like many great journeys, this tale begins with tragedy.

"Wake up!"

Alver stirred in his cot, his arms prickled with goosebumps. The cool air of winter washed over him without his blanket.

"I'm awake," he muttered. "What is it?"

Buna, Alver's wife, stood over him—the look of terror spread across her face.

"What is it?" he repeated.

"Dofri isn't in his bed."

Alver shifted his gaze past his wife to Dofri's cot on the far side of the room. Their son was not there.

"We have to go find him. Now," said Buna.

Alver sat up, putting his weight on his arms. He nodded and proceeded to get out of bed.

"Where do you think he is?" he said.

"He could be anywhere, but we should start by Sökkvabekkr. He likes to play there."

Torch in hand, Buna and Alver marched through the forest behind their home, towards the edge of the swamp calling out the name of their son. The winds of winter whipped around them, drowning out their voices. The cold pierced their thick pelts.

"What if something happened to him?" said Buna.

"He is fine," replied Alver.

Sökkvabekkr Swamp was an expansive wetland on the opposite side of the forest. It stretched for miles, butting up against the base of the massive Himinbjorg Mountain.

Alver and Buna stood at the edge of the swamp, looking past it at Himinbjorg silhouetted by the full moon. The area around them was cast in dark shadows, and the sounds of the swamp, paired with the wind, sent shivers down both their spines.

Alver lifted the torch as high he could, and the couple scanned the area around them.

"Dofri," shouted Buna.

"Dofri, where are you," shouted Alver.

"You go that way, and I'll go this way," said Buna.

"No. We should stick together."

"We'll find him quicker if we split up."

"And what if something happens to either of us? Then what?"

Buna let out a deep sigh and nodded.

Alver rested his hand on her back. "We will find him," he said.

The couple began walking along the edge of the swamp, their heads swiveling back and forth in search of their boy.

"When did you last see him?" said Alver.

"He was with both of us at dinner."

A cloud moved in front of the full moon, shadowing the couple in eerie darkness. The light from the torch seemed to do little to combat it. A wolf howled in the distance. Its proximity was unknown.

Alver and Buna slowed their movement, realizing how exposed to the elements they were and that they were no good to their son, dead. Alver passed the torch to Buna and unhitched his ax from his belt.

"Dofri," Buna called out. "Son, where are you?"

The cloud moved from the moon, and a ray of light shown on the swampy ground. A mound of fur next to a wooden shed caught the couple's attention. They ran to it and picked it up.

"This is his pelt," said Buna.

"He is okay," assured Alver.

A yelp, far off in the distance, caught the attention of the couple, shifting their gaze back into the forest from which they had come. They looked at each other.

"Please, Odin, let him be all right," whispered Buna.

"Mom," shouted Dofri from the forest. "Dad, help."

They took off running in the direction of their son's voice. The two did not say a word to each other. The only sounds were the crunching of dead brush beneath their heavy footsteps and the howling of the blisteringly cold wind. Branches snapped, their pelts tore, and as they hustled through the forest, they scraped their bodies on the brush.

"Son, we're on our way," shouted Buna.

"Mom, help. He's coming," shouted Dofri.

"Hang on, son," shouted Buna.

Buna pulled in front of Alver with the torch lighting the way. He watched her as she jumped over small pools of water and smashed through thickets. Alver followed close behind. The wolf howled again.

"He's here," shouted Dofri. "Mom, help me."

"Hold on, please. We're coming."

Space started to form between Alver and Buna, and it was not long until Alver found himself surrounded by darkness with just the flickering of Buna's torch far off in the distance.

"Buna, did you find him?" shouted Alver.

A loud gasp cut through the darkness. The torch was no longer moving. Alver quickly caught up and found Buna on her knees with her back to him. The torch was lying on the ground. Alver reconnected his ax to his belt and slowly moved toward his wife.

"Buna," he whispered. "Did you find him?"

She looked back at him with tears in her eyes.

The following morning, Alver and Buna prepared a pyre. People from the town helped place stones around the pyre in the shape of a ship.

"Are you ready?" said Alver.

Buna hugged her son, wrapped in his funerary arrangements. She picked up her boy and carried the body of young Dofri out of their home. Alver walked alongside her. Buna placed him atop the pyre and dried her tears upon her sleeve.

"Lo, there do I see my father. Lo, there do I see my mother and my sisters and my brothers," she began.

Her eyes started to water again.

"Lo, there do I see the line of my people back to the beginning. Lo, there do they call to me, they bid me take my place among them in the halls of Valhalla, where thine enemies have been vanquished, where the brave shall live forever. Nor shall we mourn but rejoice for those that have died the glorious death."

T W O

THE INNKEEPERS

Two black horses with cloaked riders approached an inn with a vacancy sign. Night had fallen, and despite the full moon casting light onto the road, the larger of the two riders had decided it safer to rest for the night. She dropped to the ground and hitched her horse to the post before moving to the other rider. She extended her hand to aid the smaller rider, but he swatted it away and jumped down unassisted.

"Hmph," said the woman.

"We don't need to rest," said the smaller rider. "I don't know why you insist we call it quits."

"Because I said so. Now hitch your horse."

Begrudgingly, the smaller rider did as he was told and followed the woman into the inn.

"Welcome," said the innkeeper.

She was a portly woman with a red face. It was clear that she had been drinking. It was a slow night, and these two were the first visitors for a while.

"How many rooms will you need, mam?" said the innkeeper.

"One room. Two beds."

The innkeeper scanned the book laid out before her and nodded.

"Your names? For the ledger."

"Skadi Hervor and my son is Bjorn."

"Right this way, Skadi and Bjorn," said the innkeeper as she scurried from behind the desk. "Erik, come fetch their luggage."

A man, who until this moment had remained out of sight, appeared from around the corner. Like the innkeeper, he, too, was portly and red-faced. He picked up the few bags that Skadi and Bjorn had brought and followed behind his wife and the mother and son as they ascended the inn's stairs.

"Will this suit you?" asked the innkeeper, directing Skadi and Bjorn's attention to a large room at the top of the stairs.

"This will do," said Skadi.

Erik entered the room and placed their luggage by each of their respective beds, and quickly exited.

"Breakfast is served at seven," said the innkeeper. "If you need anything, just ring the bell by the bed. My name is Arey."

Arey followed her husband downstairs, leaving Skadi and Bjorn alone in the large room. Bjorn stood by the window looking up at the moon, then down at the road they had traveled along.

"How much further?" Bjorn asked.

"We will be there tomorrow," said Skadi. "Are you hungry?"

"I'm fine."

"You should eat."

"I'm fine," he repeated.

Skadi watched Bjorn move from the window to his bed. He lied down with his back to his mother.

"Goodnight," she said.

He did not reply.

Not before long, she was asleep, dreaming of her life before Bjorn. It quickly became a nightmare that forced her awake. Her palms were sweaty. She wiped them dry on the comforter. The moon was still high in the sky; the morning was a long way off. She looked at Bjorn. He was fast asleep.

Skadi breathed deeply and swung her feet over the side of the bed, but before they touched the ground, something caught her attention. It was a sound—the clinking of armor or a sword. She was not quite sure. Then she heard it again. Someone was at the inn other than them and the stocky, red-faced innkeepers.

Skadi grabbed her sword and moved towards the door of their room. She placed her ear against it and could faintly hear whispering on the other side.

"It could be nothing," she said to herself.

But then . . .

"Please! No, stop," shouted Arey.

Her voice was unmistakable.

Skadi quickly moved to wake up her son. Her muscular body, moving with a graceful quickness. She shook him until his eyes opened, and with a finger over her lips, she gestured for him to grab his luggage. He quickly adorned his pelt.

"What's happening?" he whispered.

"I don't know," she said.

Skadi put her ear to the door again, but this time there was no whispering. She pried it open ever so slightly and peeked out into the hall. There was no one. Skadi looked back at Bjorn and nodded for him to follow her.

"Stay close," she said.

The two moved through the hallway towards the stairs that led to the very front of the inn. Skadi kept a hand on her sword so she could act with haste if the situation warranted it. Bjorn did the same. He, too, was armed but with a smaller sword that would not encumber his childish frame.

"Please, I told you we do not have any money," shouted Arey. "We don't get many visitors this way anymore."

Skadi saw Bjorn look in the direction of the innkeeper and saw her and her husband hogtied, surrounded by three men dressed in black.

"We should help them," Bjorn whispered to Skadi.

"Quiet," was her reply.

Skadi and Bjorn reached the bottom of the stairs. They were blocked from sight by the desk the innkeeper had been standing behind when they checked in.

"Mom. Those men look like Vikings. You know what they'll do if we don't help.

"I know what they'll do to you if we do. Let's go. They're already dead," said Skadi.

Skadi grabbed Bjorn's hand so he could not protest and pulled him out of the inn to their horses hitched to the post out front of the inn.

"Mom, we can do something," said Bjorn.

"No, we cannot."

"Mom, you're strong . . . we can—"

"Your father tried to do something, and—"

"You're a coward. I hate you."

"And I love you."

She pushed her son towards his horse.

"Get up," Skadi said.

Bjorn oscillated as his mom stood behind him.

"Now," she said.

"But."

"I will take you out of here by force, child," said Skadi.

"Mom, we can help."

"I said get up on the horse."

"Dad would fight."

"Dad . . . is not here."

Bjorn huffed and turned towards the horse. He put one foot in a stirrup and stopped.

"And I blame you for that because you can help, and you're choosing not to."

"I am choosing to save you."

She grabbed him by the back of his pelt and started to lift him onto the horse.

"Hey assholes, come pick on someone your own size," shouted Bjorn.

Skadi immediately let go and turned around. She unsheathed her sword.

"Stay behind me," she commanded.

The three men came rushing out of the inn, swords drawn. They were fearsome men, each standing over six feet tall and broad-shouldered. They all had beards that covered half their faces, and they wore armored pelts made from the hides of bears.

"So, the horses belonged to you. We assumed they were the property of the fools who ran this inn," said the leader.

"You three aren't the bravest lot, taking on elderly innkeepers."

"It's this or face the jotnar and trolls that plague this land. The Gallows God has turned his back on us," said the leader.

"Like I said, not the bravest."

"Come on, mom, we can take them," said Bjorn moving to Skadi's side.

She pushed him back behind her.

"Stay where you are, boy," she said.

"It's been a couple days since we've had a good meal," said the leader, eyeing Bjorn. "Maybe it's time for some veal."

Without hesitation, Skadi lunged for the three men. Her swordplay was stunning to watch and surely impressive to all who witnessed it. She made quick work of the two subordinates and forced the leader back through the doors of the inn. Their swords clashed as the two tussled through the small roadside establishment.

While Skadi and the remaining man fought, Bjorn disappeared inside the inn and reemerged mere seconds later with the couple following behind.

Skadi and the man exited behind the inn into a stable that housed a single, decrepit, old horse. It neighed when the two brutes came crashing through its home.

The man swung his sword, and Skadi blocked, but the shock vibrated through the blade to its hilt, breaking her grip causing the heavy weapon to fall to the muddy ground. A second swipe from the man forced her to jump back to avoid a killing blow and putting her weapon out of reach.

"When I finish with you, I'll be sending everyone here to Hel," said the man.

Skadi prepared for the man's attack. He swung, and she dodged. Things went on this way for a few minutes as Skadi searched for a way to regain her sword.

"Mom," shouted Bjorn.

Her son had arrived.

"Here."

He tossed her his sword.

It was smaller than hers, but it would have to suffice. She parried with the man, unable to get close enough for a killing blow, but Bjorn positioned himself behind the man unbeknownst to the villain, and the man fell over the small boy. Skadi seized the opportunity and plunged the sword through the man's heart. It was not a long blade, but it cut clean through the man and exited his back into the ground. The horse neighed again.

She helped her son to his feet and removed the sword from the man's chest. He gasped for air as his lungs filled with blood.

Arey and Erik joined Skadi and Bjorn behind the inn. Skadi passed the man's sword to Arey.

"Each of them had one," she said. "They're valuable. Take them and shut down this inn. It's no longer safe."

"Thank you. If it were not for you, we would certainly have been killed. It is true we don't have any money. No one travels this route anymore. They haven't for years. You were the first visitors we've had in so long," said Arey.

"Why is that?" said Bjorn.

"We don't know," said Erik. "We used to get many people going to Fensalir, but people don't go that way anymore. The town is dying."

"We'll help you bury these men, then we will be on our way," said Skadi.

"Thank you again. We are indebted to you forever."

"You are indebted to him," said Skadi pointing at Bjorn. "He saved your life. Not me."

Skadi and Bjorn departed the inn the following morning, having aided Arey and Erik in discarding the men's bodies. Neither Bjorn nor Skadi had rested as they planned; however, there was nothing they could do about that now. They had a day's ride ahead of them before they reached their destination, and Skadi did not want to be caught on the road at night nor waste another day at the inn.

"Don't ever do that again," said Skadi once they had been riding for an hour.

"Do what?" said Bjorn feigning ignorance.

"You are my responsibility, and until you are an adult, you will listen to what I have to say. Do you understand, child?"

"But we saved them."

"They were killing themselves. Midgard is not safe for humans. That is why we cluster into communities. They chose to put themselves at risk by living apart. If they do not learn from what just happened, we merely staved off the inevitable. Do you understand?"

"But you and dad—"

"Do. You. Understand?"

Bjorn slowly nodded.

"Good."

"I wish it was dad who was still here," whispered Bjorn.

Skadi glanced at her son from the corner of her eyes, but she did not let him notice.

Hours later, the mother and son arrived at the edge of a small town in the shadow of a giant mountain. People were moving about, tending to chores as the day turned to night. A man by the gate put his hand on his sword as the two approached.

"Stop right there," he said.

"We mean you no harm. We are moving home," said Skadi.

"Do you have lineage here?" said the man at the gate.

"My husband was raised here. Check your logs for the name Hervor."

The man took a minute to scan through an extensive book kept by his side.

"The Hervor line goes back quite a way. And what is your name, mam?"

"Skadi Hervor and this is my son Bjorn."

"And where is your husband, the one whose bloodline is connected to this place?"

"He is dead."

"I am sorry," said the man. "I'll have you know this town is not what it used to be. Are you sure this is where you wish to move?"

"It was my husband's last wish for us to come back here."

"Then welcome to Fensalir."

T H R E E

STARTING OVER

Skadi grabbed one of the containers of cod she had procured in the morning and took it to the hjell she had built behind their home. She sat the container down inside the hjell and started to hang each codfish from the wooden racks so the fish could dry. Skadi had not done this in years, and yet the process came back to her immediately. She was a child when she used to hang cod for her parents. She had almost forgotten it.

Just out of view, Bjorn was playing with another child from the town.

"I'm definitely a sharper shot than you. My father taught me how to shoot, and he was the best there was," said Bjorn.

"I highly doubt that. I do the hunting for my family," said Gorm.

"Prove it."

"Let me run home, and I'll be back in a second," said Gorm.

Bjorn ran around the house while Gorm was gone to see what his mother was doing.

"Where's your friend?" she said without turning around.

"He went home to get his bow," said Bjorn. "What are you doing?"

"Preparing stockfish."

"Why not buy it?" said Bjorn.

"This is more cost-effective," said Skadi. "Until I find work, we have to be more frugal."

"There aren't any jobs in town?"

"Not for my particular skill set."

She put up the last fish in the container and turned around to face her son. She knelt to be at his level.

"I know this is a change, but believe me, living here is better for both of us. It's what your father wanted, and it's what I want too," she said.

"The people here are nice enough," said Bjorn. "I think I like it here."

"I'm glad."

"Bjorn, I got it," said Gorm reappearing with his bow in hand.

"Go have fun," said Skadi.

Bjorn looked back at his mother as she returned to her work before running off with his new friend.

"See, now I'll prove to you that you can't outshoot me," said Gorm. "We'll take turns with my practice target in the woods."

"Following you," said Bjorn.

The two boys ran into the forest by the house. The sun was out, and the large mountain beyond the forest was visible save for the peak that was shrouded in clouds. The cold was biting.

"Okay, here is the challenge," said Gorm. "Each player, that's you and me, takes turns shooting. You see the numbers around the board?"

"Yes," said Bjorn.

"We'll each take three shots, and that'll be considered a round. Once a player hits three of a single number, it is owned by that player. If a player owns a number, the double and triple rings are activated, allowing you to earn double or triple the number of points per the number. Once both players have hit that number three times, it'll be considered closed, and you can no longer score on that number. Whichever of us has the highest score after all numbers have been closed is the winner. Make sense?" said Gorm.

"I got it," said Bjorn. "You come up with this yourself?"

"I did. You want to go first?"

"Sure."

Gorm passed him the bow and quiver full of arrows. He held the bow in his hand and extracted one of the arrows from the quiver. Bjorn pulled back and felt the tension in the bow. He held the arrow steady for a second, then released. He let fly the second two arrows, then put the bow down to his side.

"Wow," said Gorm.

"Told you," Bjorn said. "I learned from the best."

Skadi attached the final cod to the rack and exited the hjell. After stacking multiple containers, she moved to the front of the house. She looked around and didn't see Bjorn. A breeze washed over her that sent a shiver down her spine.

"Where did he run off to?" she whispered.

"How did you do that?" shouted Gorm. "You beat me."

"I told you I'm a good shot. My dad taught me," said Bjorn.

"He must have been a great shot," said Gorm.

"He was."

"What else are you good at? How brave are you?" said Gorm.

"The bravest," said Bjorn.

"Brave enough to explore Sökkvabekkr?"

"The swamp at the edge of town?" said Bjorn. "How is that a test of bravery?"

"No one's told you? Haven't you and your mom been here for about a month?" Gorm said.

"We have."

Gorm pulled the arrows from the target and put them in the quiver. The sun was setting, and the wind had picked up.

"This town has a secret," said Gorm. "Well, not so much a secret but rather a problem."

"And?" said Bjorn.

"I can't believe no one's said anything yet, but my mom did say the town council isn't fond of this news. She says they're covering it up but that everyone knows the truth," said Gorm.

"What are you talking about?" said Bjorn.

"Come on, let's go to the swamp, and I'll tell you there," said Gorm.

Gorm started walking, but Bjorn did not budge. Gorm stopped and looked back.

"I thought you were the bravest," said Gorm.

"Of course, I am, but . . ." said Bjorn.

"But?"

Bjorn did not move. Gorm did, and before Bjorn could decide if he wanted to follow, Gorm was out of sight.

"Damn it," whispered Bjorn before running after Gorm.

"Bjorn," Skadi shouted.

She waited for a reply, and upon hearing none went to Gorm's home to check there. He lived only minutes away in a wooden cottage with a large garden. However, due to it being winter, Gorm's parents were inside around a fire.

"I'm sorry to bother you," said Skadi. "But have you seen my son? He was playing with Gorm, and they aren't at my house anymore."

"They're gone?" said Ylfur, Gorm's mother.

"I don't want to cause a panic; I just want to find them," said Skadi.

"Muni, get up. Gorm is missing."

The woman's concern at the mere statement of Gorm being gone made Skadi start to suspect something else was going on.

"It's only been a month since the last one," said Muni. "It's too soon. I'll grab my ax."

"What is going on?" said Skadi.

"When kids go missing in Fensalir, they aren't usually found, and when they are, it isn't pretty."

"And it happens every few months," said Muni holding his ax.

Bjorn had spotted Gorm in the woods and was on his trail towards Sökkvabekkr. There were roughly twenty feet between the two boys and a few trees and bushes.

"Wait up," said Bjorn.

"Come on, Mr. Brave," shouted Gorm.

"This isn't funny," said Bjorn stepping over brush and crunching twigs beneath his feet. "I'm going to turn around."

"And miss the big reveal?" said Gorm. "The swamp is just up ahead."

Bjorn spanned the twenty feet that separated the two boys and found Gorm standing at the edge of the massive swamp.

"What is your problem?" said Bjorn.

"You and your mother moved here ignorant of this town's darkness because your father was born here?"

"It was my mother's idea," said Bjorn.

Gorm turned his back to Bjorn to look out over the expansive wetland.

"You see that mountain in the distance? That's Himinbjorg. Supposedly its peak stretches into Asgard and is home to Heimdall. Heimdall sees all things, but he must not see what happens here; otherwise, why would he allow Odin to let us suffer?"

"What are you talking about?"

Gorm turned around to face Bjorn.

"One month ago, a boy was found out here. His parents had been searching for him because he wasn't the only child to go missing in the past few months," said Gorm.

"Kids go missing all the time," said Bjorn. "My mother and father and I came across many parents who had lost their children when we traveled."

"But the couple found their child," said Gorm. "But he was missing his . . ."

Gorm knelt in the swamp.

"Missing his what?"

Gorm fumbled with something just out of sight of Bjorn. Bjorn moved closer to see what he was doing.

"What was he missing?"

"His . . . heart," said Gorm turning around and smearing Bjorn with mud.

Gorm let out a huge laugh, and Bjorn pushed him down.

"What's wrong with you?"

"Boys," shouted Skadi.

She emerged from the tree line with Muni and Ylfur.

"What's going on here?" said Ylfur.

"Mom. I'm sorry," said Gorm.

"Let's go. Now," said Muni.

"We're sorry for what he did," said Ylfur to Skadi before yanking her son by his arm and dragging him back into the forest.

"What were you thinking?" said Skadi to Bjorn.

"Nothing," he replied, wiping the mud from his body.

"It'll be nightfall soon. Let's return home."

Bjorn moved ahead of his mother, who did a full circle before following her son. Skadi took one step and stopped. Quickly she looked back, and very far in the distance, hidden behind tall grass protruding from the water, she saw the silhouette of a man descend beneath the water.

Above her, out of her view, was a woman looking down at her and Bjorn.

"She is the one," whispered the woman.

F O U R

THE GUEST

Skadi stayed on guard through the night, thinking about what she saw in the swamp and what Gorm's parents told her about the town's children. She had already decided that Fensalir was possibly a mistake but did not yet know where would make a smarter alternative.

She fetched a map of Midgard from the closet and laid it out on the dining room table. She scanned over it, pointing at various towns that she and her husband had visited before they had Bjorn. None would suit her and Bjorn now. But as she began her second pass of the map, a town presented itself as a solution.

"Thrymheim," she said.

Skadi was standing by the stove when Bjorn emerged from his room to find the cottage packed up. Though there was not much, all their belongings were assembled by the door, and they were prepared to be situated on their horses. She watched him scan the home with bewilderment spread across his face.

"What is going on?" he said.

"We are leaving for Thrymheim," she said.

"Why?" said Bjorn.

"Because I said so."

"But I don't want to leave."

"You protested coming here, and now you want to stay?" said Skadi.

"I would rather be here than Thrymheim," said Bjorn.

"Why?" she said.

"Because that's where you are from," said Bjorn. "And I would rather be where dad is from, even if someone is killing kids."

Skadi slapped Bjorn.

"Do you hate me so much that you would risk your life to spite me?" she said.

Bjorn ground his teeth and attempted to run from the home, but Skadi grabbed him by the arm and yanked his small body back in front of her. She knelt to be at his eye level.

"Listen, child," she said. "I will not tolerate this foolishness. It is just you and me in this world, and we did not make that decision. Your father did when he did what he did. When you become an adult, you will be free to make your own decisions and live how you wish. I promise I will not do anything to stop you, but until then, you are my responsibility, and because of that, we are moving to Thrymheim."

"Mom, you are strong. I know this. You know this. The people here need our help, but you would rather focus solely on me. You're a skilled warrior, and I am the sharpest shot of anyone I have ever met. Whatever it is that's killing these kids, we can probably do something about it, but instead, you choose to leave. Dad wouldn't leave them. He'd try and do something," said Bjorn.

"Your father was a brave man. There is no denying that. But your father thought it was possible to be decent in an indecent world. Midgard is messy, and it requires hard decisions."

"You're not making a hard decision, mom. You are making an easy one. It's easy to choose your child over others'. And you know that."

"What would you have us do? Investigate the slain children? Root out who the killer is and put them down?" said Skadi.

"Yes," Bjorn said.

"We set out for Thrymheim in an hour," said Skadi.

Bjorn stomped his foot.

"Stop," said Skadi."

A knock at the door distracted the mother and son. Bjorn was first to react.

"I'll get it," he said.

Skadi grabbed him by the shoulder and stood up.

"Who is it?" she said.

"My name is Frija. May I have a moment?"

"Now isn't a good time," said Skadi.

"It will only be a minute," said Frija.

Skadi opened the door to their home but did not let the mysterious woman enter.

"What is it?" said Skadi.

"You're not wrong to want to leave, but your son is right. You can help the people here," said Frija.

"Leave," said Skadi.

"Please, just a moment."

"Who are you?" said Skadi.

"I have lived in Fensalir for a long time," said Frija. "I've seen this town have its ups and its downs, but this has been the longest dark period I have ever seen, but I know that you can do something about it."

"I need you to go," said Skadi.

She moved to slam the door, but Frija caught it and held it open. She was unnaturally strong, and the door would not budge.

"What's going on here?" said Skadi. "How are you . . ."

"Think about why you came here," said Frija. "You want a stable life for you and your son but the one place in Midgard where you can provide that life needs help."

Frija released the door.

"I'll come by again in an hour. That should give you time to decide if you would rather fight to save the people of Fensalir or flee to Thrymheim."

Skadi closed the door to their home and turned to face Bjorn.

"How did she know you wanted to go to Thrymheim?" said Bjorn.

"She must have been spying on us. Even more reason for us to leave," said Skadi.

Another knock on the door. Skadi answered.

"It's only been a minute," she said.

"What?" said Ylfur.

"Sorry. I thought you were someone else."

"We wanted to give you this as a token of gratitude for coming to get us last night," said Ylfur, handing over a basket of individual honey nut cakes. "Muni thinks these are the best thing I make. Enjoy."

"You didn't have to do this," said Skadi.

"We know, but we wanted to. It's the least we can do. Ever since this began, the whole town has been on edge. Everyone only worries about themselves," said Ylfur.

"How come no one has done anything?" said Skadi.

"The town council is in on it. I know they are," said Ylfur.

"Ylfur," said Muni. "That's just a rumor and a bad one."

"They are. I know they are. They don't want to acknowledge it's happening. They didn't even come to that poor boy's pyre last month. They used to come to even the most mundane funerals, but they didn't show for Dofri's. Why is that? Ashamed?" she said.

"We don't know that," said Muni.

"You don't know that, but I do. The town council blocks any attempt at solving these crimes, and they've gotten rich because of it. It's a conspiracy," said Ylfur.

"I see," said Skadi.

"Why was the boy's heart missing?" said Bjorn.

"I don't know. The bodies that have been found have always been mutilated like that. It is a horrible thing that happened. I'm sorry," said Ylfur.

"Anyway, I hope you enjoy the cakes," said Muni.

"We will," replied Skadi and closed the door after the couple left.

Bjorn immediately took one of the cakes and stuffed it in his mouth. His eyes lit up as he chewed.

"They're good," he said through a mouth full of food.

Skadi looked past her son at her sword leaning against the wall.

"Put those in the kitchen. Let's take a walk," said Skadi.

Bjorn grabbed one more cake and put the rest in the kitchen as instructed. The mother and son departed their home a minute later.

"Where are we going?" said Bjorn.

"To the council hall in the center of town," said Skadi.

"They are busy," said a woman when Skadi and Bjorn arrived at the door of the council hall.

"Too busy to discuss what's been happening around here?" said Skadi.

"Ylfur told you the town council doesn't concern itself with our plight," said Frija, who had appeared behind Skadi and Bjorn as they pleaded with the defiant guard.

"Who are you? What do you want with us?" said Skadi.

"Not here," said Frija.

Frija began walking away from Skadi and Bjorn. Skadi looked at her son then followed. Bjorn brought up the rear.

Frija took the two across town to a small cottage where a fire had warmed the interior, and it smelled of sweet baked goods and tea. She offered whatever they desired to Skadi and Bjorn, but Skadi declined and patted Bjorn's hand when he stuck it out for some cake.

"You've had enough already," she said.

"Please take a seat. I have a story to tell."

FIVE

FRIJA'S STORY

Years Ago

"You folks sit up here and dictate what you think is best for us, and we are just supposed to go along with it. But I'm telling you that I have had enough. We all have had enough," said Abel, one of the many townsfolk who had come to the monthly public council meeting.

"He's right. This new rune fee is absurd," said Rindr, another resident of Fensalir. "Do you know how many people live in poverty? We cannot afford this."

"We're already taxed higher than most of the surrounding towns, and now you want to tack on a rune fee," said Svala. "You're just lining your own pockets."

"I have already said that this is a mandated and quite frankly necessary investment, and the cost is being borne mostly by our wealthiest residents. These runes have not been maintained for years, and the strength of their magic is waning. If they diminish entirely, we could be overrun with jotnar or trolls, or Odin forbid, we could be visited by a dark elf," said Dana Robert, Leader of the town council.

"Dana is right," said Elfr Rói, one of five council members. "We are looking at decades of deferred upkeep that is finally starting to rear its ugly head, and if we do not act now, we will be facing a catastrophe. Has anyone here ever seen what a troll that wanders into a town can do to that town? I'm talking about just one troll. It's a slaughter. These runes keep that from happening."

"And why weren't they maintained? Whose fault is that? It's not ours," said Svala.

"No, it's not your fault, but we have to deal with it," said Liótr Goti, another council member. "If we don't make this investment now, we will be looking at serious trouble in only a matter of years."

"The trouble is already here," said Abel. "It arrived when we elected you five to lead this town."

"We are doing this because someone had to step up. If you don't like how we are doing things, then run for my seat in four years when I'm up for reelection. We don't want to have to make these decisions, but someone has to," said Petronilla Wilde. "My colleagues told you we are facing a potential catastrophe, and unfortunately, it is going to cost all of us something to fix."

The audience erupted into a mass of people talking. Dana pounded her gavel three times, and the crowd quieted.

"We understand that this new fee is undesired and that a large percentage of this town is impoverished. That is why we are conducting these informational hearings so we can listen to your concerns," said Dana.

"Save it. We already know you've made up your mind," said Rindr.

"That's it. This meeting is adjourned," said Dana.

She pounded the gavel another three times, and the five council members all stood in unison.

"See, look, folks. They didn't hear what they wanted to hear, so they're leaving. They thought we would just take this lying down," said Abel.

In a private room, closed off to the public, the five council members took a seat around a large wooden desk with runic carvings all over.

"The people of this town are fools," said Lofn Lamont. "How can they not see that this is in their best interest?"

"Most of those people out there probably didn't even vote anyway. If you don't vote, you shouldn't have a say," said Elfr.

"I agree," said Liótr.

"Council members," said Dana. "We have to remember that despite their frustrations, we are here to do a job. Let us do that job."

"We're here to represent the people," said Petronilla. "But what do we do when their wants conflict with their needs?"

"We make the hard decisions. That's why we are here," said Dana.

"That sounds nice, but what do we get out of it?" said Lofn. "This is an unpaid position, and last I checked, all we get is grief for whatever we do even if it is good in the long term."

Dana stood up and walked to Lofn.

"I understand," she said. "But we live in this town, too, and a troll doesn't know if they're stepping on a council member or a fisherman. We will all be crushed by the monsters of Midgard if we let them cross into Fensalir."

"Not all monsters," said Elfr.

"What was that?" said Dana.

"I said not all monsters will crush us," he said.

All the council members turned their attention to Elfr.

"We make decisions to keep the town safe from things that go bump in the night, and how are we repaid? They tell us that we are lining our own pockets. Tell me. Petronilla, have you ever taken a bribe?" said Elfr.

"No," she said.

"What about you, Liótr? Anyone ever pay you for a political favor?" said Elfr.

"Not once," said Liótr.

"We are honest men and women, and yet we are not treated as such. Wouldn't there be some justice if at least we got a little bit for ourselves if we're going to be accused of it anyway?" said Elfr.

"Easy, Elfr," said Dana. "Where are you going with this?"

"All I'm saying is that we deserve it. We've been in office for two years, and this town hasn't had a raid since, thanks to our decision to hire more guards to tend to the boundaries. Illnesses are down, thanks to our mandatory health checkups. That was your idea, Dana. We've done all of this, and the people who live here think we are lining our pockets. Let that sink in. All because we are asking them to pay a little more each month for something that will keep the evils of Midgard at bay," Elfr said.

"This is a very dangerous line of thinking," said Dana.

"I'm okay with it," said Lofn.

Dana looked at her.

"I'm okay with it too," said Liótr.

"Me as well," said Petronilla.

"What about you, Dana?" said Elfr.

The Council Leader oscillated for a moment, then got up from her seat next to Lofn.

"We are here to protect the people," she said. "That's what we were elected to do."

"And we still will, but we'll be getting a little compensation for it," said Elfr.

"It won't be money," said Dana.

"We're aware," said Elfr.

"I'm assuming you were all visited then?" said Dana.

"He showed up last night," said Lofn.

"He said he would give us all gifts but only if we all agreed," said Petronilla.

"And do we all agree?" said Dana.

In unison, the four other council members said "yes."

"Then who am I to stand in the way?" said Dana.

At that moment, the door to the council chamber opened. A cold wind swept through the room, sending shivers down each council member's back. Standing in the doorway was a shadowy entity with the figure of a man. He stepped forward, and the doors closed behind him.

Dana Robert took her seat at the head of the table and gestured for their guest to be seated at the opposite end.

"Please, sir. Have a seat," said Dana.

"I'm glad to see you have all taken my offer seriously," said the visitor.

The following night, a young child named Ake was playfully trekking into the woods. The sun was setting, and her parents had called twice for her to come inside, but she was too obsessed with her wooden dolls and a whisper that caught her attention.

She stepped over branches and fallen leaves, playing with her dolls as she did so. They were on an epic adventure in search of the source of this mysterious whisper.

"Who is there?" she called out more than once. "I'll find you."

But even as she grew nervous and the twilight turned to darkness, she continued. Her parents had raised her to be brave after all.

Before long, she was deep in the woods, surrounded by trees and far from civilization (for a child). Fensalir proper was at least a ten-minute walk, but she did not know in what direction. As soon as she realized she did not know her location, Ake started to panic. She put the dolls down at her side and spun around, looking for a way out.

"Mom," she shouted.

The whisper she had been following answered, "over here."

Ake's heartbeat quickened, and her palms turned sweaty.

"Mom, come get me, please," shouted Ake.

"Your mother is not here," said the whisper.

It was right behind her. Ake turned around and standing over her was an immense figure shadowed by the dark of night. It had the outline of a man, but its fingers were like claws, and horns protruded from its forehead. The figure knelt to be at her level and grabbed little Ake by the shoulder.

"You are the first," whispered the creature, and it stabbed one of its claw-like fingers through little Ake's chest.

The five members of the town council were witnesses to Ake's death. They had been just out of view for the child, but they saw it all. It sickened some, but it did not change the mind of any. They had made their deal, and this was the price.

SIX

THE JOURNEY BEGINS

The Present:

"Ake's body was found the next day. Her parents had a funeral pyre for her. It was well attended by the people of Fensalir. Afterward, a somber mood overcame the town, and resistance to the rune fee died with the child. It went into effect without any pushback. But it was too late. The council members had already let the monster in, and it had claimed its first victim," said Frija.

Skadi stood up when Frija finished talking. She walked around the cottage and stopped by the stove with her back to Frija and Bjorn. She turned around and looked deeply at both.

"What was it they made a deal with?" she said.

"The creature is a jötunn. It feeds on children, and in exchange for the sole rights to this town, it granted each of the council members a special gift."

"What gift?" said Skadi.

"Using seidr magic, it granted each council member an ability. To Lofn Lamont, the jötunn gave her the power to bring the dead back to life as personal servants. She is now a necromancer."

"The others?" said Skadi.

"Petronilla Wilde was given the power of invisibility. She serves as the council's spy. Liótr Goti was given demi-god-like strength. Elfr Rói was given the ability to control minds but only the minds of fools and beasts."

"And the Council Leader?" said Skadi.

"That one, I do not know. I've never seen her use it."

Skadi sat down again. For a minute, the room was quiet. The sweet smell of cakes and tea still permeated the room, but something else trumped the joy they brought. The feeling of dread that had seeped into the three negated that joy.

Finally, Skadi spoke.

"You brought us here to tell us this because you want us to do something about it? Is that it?" said Skadi.

"I brought you here because I want you, Skadi, to do something about it, but if you wish to bring your boy along for the journey, I will not stop you," said Frija.

Skadi looked at Bjorn.

"What choice do I have? I can't leave him here without me. But let me ask you something before I commit to anything I'm sure to regret. Why me?"

"The jötunn is not the only practitioner of seidr magic in Fensalir. I have seen that a savior will come, and I believe that savior is you. But I warn you that a vision is not guaranteed to pass. I am asking you to do something dangerous for the people of this town," said Frija.

"I'm not doing this for the people of this town. I'm doing it for him," said Skadi pointing at Bjorn. "He needs a place to grow up safely, and it was his father's wish it be Fensalir."

"Whatever motivates you as long as the outcome is the right one," said Frija.

"Where do I begin?" Skadi said.

"You are strong," said Frija. "Unfortunately, the council members and the jötunn are stronger. You will need to exceed their strength if you are to free this town."

"And how am I to do that?" said Skadi.

"By ingesting the roots of Yggdrasil. There are three locations in Midgard where a mortal can access the roots. Those are Urðarbrunnr, Hvergelmir, and Mímisbrunnr. I'll provide you with a map. Visit each location, take a piece of Yggdrasil for yourself and Bjorn, if you like, and consume it. Doing so will give you the strength to defeat the council and the jötunn," said Frija.

Bjorn stood up and walked over to his mother.

"We can do this," he said.

She looked her son in the eyes and said, "I know."

Outside of the cottage, a woman was standing by the window. She pressed her ear against it; however, she was not visible to Frija, Bjorn, or Skadi inside. Her body was completely transparent.

"You won't do a damn thing," whispered the woman.

After Frija provided her with the map, Skadi and Bjorn departed the cottage for their home on the other side of town.

"I know you don't want to do this, mom," said Bjorn. "But I'm happy that you decided to help."

"I'm not doing anything," said Skadi. "We are going to Thrymheim tonight."

"But you told Frija . . . ," said Bjorn.

"I told her what she wanted to hear," said Skadi.

"Mom," shouted Bjorn.

"Listen, child."

She turned to face him and put her hand on his shoulder.

"There is much about the world that you don't know. Frija was lying," said Skadi.

"How do you know?" Bjorn said.

"I will show you at home."

Upon arriving at home, Skadi proceeded to grab a map she kept stored in a compartment in the kitchen. She laid it down, side by side, to the map Frija had given her.

"You see here, here, and here?" said Skadi pointing at three locations on her map.

"Yes," said Bjorn.

"Those should correlate with here, here, and here," Skadi said, pointing to the corresponding locations on Frija's map.

"They don't?" said Bjorn.

"Look closely, son. The landmasses on her map are not on mine. Those areas do not exist in Midgard."

"How do you know your map is trustworthy?" said Bjorn.

"Because it has been used extensively by your father and I."

Bjorn examined Frija's map then looked at his mother's map. His mother's map appeared weathered by years of use. She wasn't lying about the extent to which it had been a guide for her and his father.

"There is another thing Frija said that I do not trust," said Skadi. "In all my years, I have never heard of a jötunn being able to use seidr magic to give humans the power of demi-gods. They're just not that powerful of creatures. Elves, sure. Gods, of course, but a jötunn? Not possible."

"Why would she lie?" said Bjorn.

"That isn't our concern because we are leaving," said Skadi.

"Mom, you just don't want to help. Dad would—" said Bjorn.

"How many times am I going to have to tell you, child? Your dad is not here, I am, and what I say is what we do. Now pack up your belongings. We have a long journey ahead of us," Skadi shouted.

That evening, Skadi and Bjorn sat down to what they suspected would be their last meal in Fensalir. After a short month in the swamp-side town that existed in the shadow of Himinbjorg Mountain, the two were going to depart for Thrymheim on the other end of Midgard.

The mother and son ate in silence. The crackling fire of the stove provided the only sound. Skadi refilled her bowl with the stew she had prepared and, upon noticing Bjorn's bowl was empty, handed him the ladle. He waved it away, and she sat it on the table.

"We'll leave at midnight. I suggest you be rested and full," she said.

"Leaving like cowards," whispered Bjorn.

Skadi did not respond and simply consumed her second bowl of stew in quiet. When she finished, she rose and headed to bed.

"Make sure you are rested," she repeated and disappeared inside her bedroom.

Bjorn put down his food and took his knife from his pouch. He observed the initials carved in the handle.

"Lo, there do I see my father," he whispered.

Later, Skadi startled awake. She was in a cold sweat, and goosebumps had formed up and down both of her arms. The door to her bedroom was open and cold air was rushing in. She moved to close it and saw the front door to their home was open as well.

"Bjorn," she said.

Someone hit her in the back of the head and her vision went blurry. She fell to her hands and knees and touched the back of her head. There was blood pooling in her hair.

She looked back. There was no one.

"Who's there?" she shouted.

A second blow arrived on her upper back, forcing her flat on the ground. Her head and back throbbed, but she had felt worse pain and could manage. She rolled to her side and felt her legs brush against the legs of someone who couldn't possibly be there.

"Petronilla," she whispered.

"In the flesh," said a bodiless voice.

A third blow landed on Skadi's stomach. That one really hurt. Skadi curled up into the fetal position as the invisible woman pelted her with subsequent blows. The beating stopped and for a second Skadi thought the woman had left, but then she felt hands around her neck.

She spit blood, and it coated the face of Petronilla, outlining her features in crimson.

"Boo," whispered Petronilla.

Skadi responded with a headbutt to Petronilla's face, knocking the invisible woman off.

"Mom, what's happening?" shouted Bjorn, appearing in the doorway after hearing the commotion.

"Grab my sword," shouted Skadi as she quickly rose to her feet.

A strike caught Skadi's left cheek. She ate the hit and held her ground.

"Mom, here," shouted Bjorn.

Skadi reached behind her to take the sword while keeping her gaze forward. Petronilla had been quick to wipe the blood from her face and, in the dark of night, was near impossible to detect.

Skadi swung the sword, and though it was a skillful swipe, she hit nothing but air.

"You missed," taunted Petronilla.

Skadi kept up her attack, but swing after swing resulted in nothing but misses.

"Frustrating, isn't it?" said Petronilla right before she swept Skadi's legs out from under her.

Skadi hit the ground hard. To add insult to injury, Petronilla kicked her in the face, bloodying her nose.

"And she thinks you can defeat all of us?" said Petronilla. "I'll have you know I am the weakest."

Petronilla moved to kick Skadi again, but she caught her foot.

"You didn't have to tell me you were the weakest," said Skadi. "Children hit harder."

She grappled with Petronilla's leg and took the invisible woman to the ground. They wrestled, and even without being able to see her, Skadi could feel out her prey and, within seconds, pinned her. She put her in a headlock and cut off her airflow.

Petronilla thrashed about, but Skadi's grip was powerful, and within seconds she was unconscious.

"Bjorn, get the rope from out back."

Moments later, he returned with a spare rope Skadi used in the hjell to hang the fish. Skadi felt out Petronilla's arms and legs and hogtied her as tightly as she could. When she was confident that Petronilla could not get free, Skadi stepped back.

A splash of water to where Skadi suspected Petronilla's face to be, woke up the invisible woman.

"I'm awake," she shouted.

"You should have slit our throats in our sleep," said Skadi. "You're a fool."

"Let me go," pleaded Petronilla.

"What are you?" said Skadi.

"Human," replied Petronilla.

"Bullshit."

"If you let me go, I can introduce you to him. You think you can protect your boy now? Imagine what you could do with his blessing?" said Petronilla.

"I hope you know I can't let you live," said Skadi.

"If you let me live, I'll . . ." said Petronilla.

"Bjorn step out," said Skadi.

He nodded and closed the bedroom door behind him.

Skadi knelt to be at Petronilla's level. She felt out the woman's mouth and placed her left hand over it.

"It is surreal to feel you tremble and not see you," said Skadi as she put a knife to Petronilla's neck.

Despite being muffled, Petronilla pleaded for her life.

Skadi pressed the knife into her flesh, drawing the first drop of blood.

"Tell me where the jötunn is," she said.

Petronilla dropped the invisibility, revealing a weathered face with greying hair.

"I will."

Skadi followed behind a bound Petronilla through the forest. They had left Bjorn at home hidden in a secret compartment beneath the kitchen floor in case any other visitors decided to drop in unannounced. The moon was high up in the sky, and the nighttime clouds cast shadows on the forest floor.

"How much further?" said Skadi.

"Not much. He resides just up this way," said Petronilla.

A clearing was beginning to emerge, and so was Sökkvabekkr beyond it.

"He's here," said Petronilla.

A swish cut through the forest and stifled yelp caused Petronilla to turn around in a panic. Skadi was gone.

"Hello?" said Petronilla.

Frija held Skadi down with a hand over her mouth.

"Are you a fool?" whispered Frija.

Frija kept Skadi down and put a finger to her lips.

"Do not speak," she whispered.

Skadi looked up at Petronilla and saw the silhouette of a man with horns and claws for hands standing over her.

"Quietly and slowly move with me in the opposite direction," whispered Frija.

Skadi nodded and got up once Frija let her free. She kept an eye on the silhouetted figure standing over Petronilla, and her heart sank.

Petronilla was alone, standing at the edge of the swamp where many children had been found dead over the years. Skadi had bound her arms behind her back. Invisibility or not, she was defenseless. A chill swept over the land; Petronilla shivered, and her heartbeat hastened.

"You would lead someone here who means to do me harm?" said the jötunn in a bellowing voice.

"Please, sir, I'm sorry. I knew you would kill her. That's the only reason I led her here," said Petronilla.

"If I'm to do your job, then what is the purpose of you?" said the creature.

"I don't know," said Petronilla staring down at the ground.

The creature grabbed her chin with his left hand and forced her to look up at him. His eyes glowed red, and Petronilla's entire body trembled violently.

"I'm sorry," she said.

"Not yet, you aren't," said the creature.

Skadi and Frija both looked back when they heard the scream.

"We should go for her," said Skadi.

"She's dead," said Frija. "And you will be too if you go back there. I told you what you need to do. Why didn't you listen?"

"I . . . I didn't believe you," said Skadi.

"You need to set off on your quest. The people of Fensalir need you. Don't make stupid mistakes like this again," said Frija.

Dana Robert looked over the remains of Petronilla Wilde as the light faded from her eyes. She shook her head in disappointment.

"What's her name?" said Dana.

"Ska . . . di," Petronilla said with her dying breath.

SEVEN

THE VISITOR

A bearded man with long, flowing hair and a scar covering the right side of his face approached a vacant inn. Dressed in a brown and grey, armored pelt made from bear hide, he kept a massive ax fastened to his back. The man stood over six and a half feet tall, had broad shoulders, and a weathered demeanor. He was older but physically very imposing.

Storm clouds spiraled in the night sky, and lightning struck as the door to the inn opened.

"A room," said the man.

Arey was standing behind the desk as the man entered. She had the inn's ledger in her hand.

"Welcome," she said.

The man said nothing.

"A room. Right. Would you please sign the . . ." said Arey.

The man looked at her, and Arey quickly sat the ledger down.

"Never mind," she said. "Right this way."

The man followed her up the stairs to the first room on the right.

"Will this be sufficient?" she said.

The man nodded.

"If you need anything, just—"

The door slammed in her face.

"Okay then," she said and proceeded back down the stairs.

"Who was that?" said Erik.

She shrugged her shoulders.

"I think we should have heeded that woman's advice," said Arey. "He looks like another ruffian."

"What should we do?" said Erik.

"We haven't had an incident since those three men showed up last month, let's not get paranoid. Maybe he just wants to be left alone," she said.

"And maybe he wants to rob us," said Erik.

The husband and wife peeked up the stairs at the man's room.

"Take the swords out back and put them in the wagon. If they're worth money like the woman said they are, we can sell them in Fensalir," said Arey.

"What will you do?" said Erik.

"Nothing. Yet," replied Arey.

The man removed the ax and leaned it against the bedside table, then disrobed. He had been traveling for almost two days without rest since hearing word that his partners had come this way. In less than a minute, his eyes were closed.

He awoke to a loud crash outside his bedroom window. Groggily he waded over to the window to see what the commotion was. Erik had dropped the swords. The torrential downfall had made the ground slick with mud.

"What is that fool doing?" whispered the man.

He adorned his armored pelt, grabbed his ax, and headed downstairs.

"May I help you, sir?" said Arey.

"Those swords your . . . ?" asked the man.

"Husband," said Arey.

"Your husband was carrying—where did he get them?" the man said.

"What swords?" she said.

The man placed a hand on Arey's shoulder. It was rough with calluses and scars.

"Do I look like a fool?" he said.

She shook her head.

"Then do not lie again."

Arey's heart was pounding, and a cold sweat formed on her brow.

She breathed deeply and said, "They were left here by accident. A visitor forgot them."

"I told you not to lie," said the man as he tightened the grip on Arey's shoulder.

The pain was localized but tremendous, and immediately her eyes started to water.

"I know the owners of those swords," said the man. "Where are my men?"

The man watched as Erik scrambled to gather the swords and hide them in the shed behind the inn. His presence startled Erik, and he fell back into the door.

"What's going on here?" he said.

"Give him the swords," said Arey.

The man observed Erik as he looked at his wife then up at him. There was no confusing who the alpha was of the three. Erik balled a fist, then spun around and opened the shed.

"They're yours," said Erik offering up the three swords.

The man pushed Arey out of his way and stepped forward. He grabbed just one of the swords from Erik and inspected it closely.

"This belonged to a man named Ragi Julfr. Where is he?"

Erik and Arey locked eyes.

"He's dead," said Arey. "It happened just about a month ago. A woman came here with her son, and when your men tried to rob my husband and I, she rescued us. I'm sorry. Please don't kill us."

"Who?" shouted the man, his voice bellowing and deep.

"I have her name written in our ledger. Please let me get it, and I will show you."

The man followed Arey and Erik inside the inn and out of the heavy rain. Shaking, Arey grabbed the book by the front desk and opened it to the page with the most recent visitor entry.

"Her name was . . ." said Arey.

She scanned down the page.

"Quickly," said the man.

"Skadi. She had a boy with her named Bjorn," said Arey.

"Skadi Hervor?" said the man.

"Yes," said Arey.

"Where did they go?" he said.

"The nearest town is Fensalir. The only people who stay here are going there," said Arey.

"Then I am close. I came to this part of Midgard looking for my men who abandoned me. Skadi did me a favor. Keep their swords, but I will be on my way."

The man handed over the one sword he'd been holding and made for the door of the inn.

"We're in troubling times. It's ill-advised that you operate an inn in such a remote location. Midgard isn't what it used to be," said the man.

"We're aware," said Arey.

The man closed the door behind him just as thunder reverberated through the inn.

"We are definitely leaving this time," said Erik.

"I know," said Arey.

Though he had chosen to stop at this inn for his first full night's sleep in two days, the man mounted his horse with only a few minutes of rest because the knowledge of Skadi being so close had provided him with a second wind. The rainfall had not let up, and his body was weary, but he persisted on to the town of Fensalir. He was only hours away from a woman he had not seen in years.

EIGHT

IN ROUTE TO URÐARBRUNNR

Frija put her hands out in front of Skadi, palms upward.

"Take my hands," she said.

Skadi hesitated, then placed her hands in Frija's.

A warm glow emanated from Frija's body and transferred to Skadi's. Immediately the wounds she had sustained during her brief bout with Petronilla healed. Frija broke the connection once Skadi was back to full health.

"Take care on the road. The journey ahead of you is dangerous and will not be easy, but if you are successful, so many lives will be spared," said Frija.

"Why can't you come with us?" said Bjorn.

Skadi turned to her son.

"You're not coming with me," she said. "I want you to stay with her."

"Mom, you can't do this by yourself. You need me with you," said Bjorn.

"I brought you here to protect you, and jötunn or not, you are safer with Frija than you are with me on a treacherous journey."

"Actually, that is not the case," said Frija. "My intervention in the affairs of this town has certainly raised a few eyebrows. I'm going to be a target here."

"Then join us," repeated Bjorn.

"Unfortunately, I cannot do that. . . . My role here is to simply put you on the path. It's entirely up to you to walk it," said Frija.

Skadi looked at Bjorn.

"Gather your bow and quiver, son," said Skadi.

Bjorn nodded.

Skadi turned to Frija.

"I brought my son here to keep him safe, and right away, we must venture back out into Midgard. If this turns out to be an elaborate trick, there is nowhere in the nine realms you will be able to hide to save you from my vengeance," said Skadi.

"I know. I am asking you to do this fully aware of your past Skadi Hervor," said Frija. "It is that fire in you that makes me believe you will succeed."

The mother and son bid Frija farewell and set off once again into the land of lawlessness that existed between towns and settlements. Hours later, they passed the inn they spent part of a night a month ago.

"I heard what Frija said," said Bjorn. "What did she mean about your past?"

"That's a story for another time."

Bjorn looked at the ground ahead of his horse. He then perked up, having remembered something his friend once said.

"Have you ever seen a dragon? Gorm told me that his uncle saw a dragon once. He said he was only feet away."

"That's a lie," said Skadi.

"How do you know?"

"Because no one survives an encounter with a dragon," said Skadi.

"Is that why you think Midgard is so dangerous?"

"No."

"Why?" Bjorn said.

"Midgard is dangerous because it is dangerous," said Skadi.

"That's not an answer," said Bjorn.

Bjorn watched his mother look away from him and up at the clouded peak of Himinbjorg Mountain. Heimdall was somewhere up there looking down on Midgard. He hoped he was looking down on them.

"Keep an eye on us," he whispered.

The two rode in silence for the next few hours as the sun peaked and then descended. Skadi steered her horse off the road, and Bjorn followed.

"Let's set up camp here and eat," she said.

Bjorn helped pull together a fire, and the two consumed dried cod that they had brought from home.

"In the morning, we'll not stop until we reach Hlíðarendi. There we will stock up for the long journey to Urðarbrunnr," said Skadi.

Bjorn nodded and finished his fish.

The sun set entirely, and the quiet allowed for a peaceful Midgardian night. Stars shone brightly in the sky. The only sound was that of the crackling fire.

Bjorn lay on his back, staring up at the stars. Skadi sat up opposite him with her sword resting next to her.

"Rest your eyes, Bjorn. I will keep watch," she said.

It was not long before he dozed off.

Bjorn awoke to the cracking of tree branches and clanging of metal against stone. The campfire was snuffed under a mound of dirt. Quickly Bjorn realized blood drenched his pelt. He checked for injuries, but the blood was not his own. Bjorn looked left and saw his horse ripped in two. The upper half was lying by him and the bottom half on the other side of the road.

Startled, he jumped to his feet, spun around, looking in all directions. The sound of wood splintering and metal clashing reverberated from within the forest that lined the road. Bjorn checked for his mother. She was gone.

"Mom," he shouted.

"Stay where you are," she shouted back.

"Where are you?" he shouted.

A tree crashed. Bjorn saw the leaves descend and started running in that direction. He quickly stopped, ran back to the smothered campfire, and grabbed his quiver and bow.

Skadi ducked under a boulder that came flying over her head. It crashed behind her, snapping a few smaller trees as it rolled through the dense forest. Before she had a chance to retaliate, she had to sidestep to avoid a smaller but faster-moving boulder that lodged into the trunk of a tree behind her.

A mighty roar sounded through the forest, and hot breath washed over Skadi like a strong breeze. A third boulder flew her way and landed only feet ahead of her but had enough momentum that she had to jump over it, so it did not crush her.

Skadi pivoted and began running deeper into the forest. She heard powerful footsteps that shook the ground following her. They were booming and fast-paced. She just barely kept enough distance to stay out of reach.

Bjorn heard his mother, and whatever it was she was facing getting farther and farther away. They were faster than him, and he wasn't keeping pace even though he was giving it his all. He reached the place where they had been and saw the clearing their fight had created. Everywhere there were boulders and splintered trees. The creature's giant footprints decorated the muddy ground.

"Mom!" he shouted.

The clash of metal against stone rang out. Bjorn took off in the direction of the sound. Whatever it was that his mother was facing was ferocious and powerful. He could sense the intensity of their battle without seeing it. He knew she needed help and sooner rather than later.

"Mom, I'm coming," he shouted.

Skadi struck a rock thrown at her and redirected it over a cliff. She had reached a dead-end in the forest and was quickly running out of options. Behind her, she faced a cliff, and ahead of her, she faced . . .

"A troll," shouted Bjorn, finally having caught up to his mother.

"I told you to stay where you are," she shouted.

The troll looked back at the boy and grinned, baring its yellow teeth. It was a massive creature, standing over twelve feet tall with a twelve-foot wingspan. Its biceps were fifty inches around, and its waist was double that. The troll's skin was grey, and the sclera of its eyes were yellow like its teeth. Covering its hands was the blood of Bjorn's horse.

"Mom," shouted Bjorn.

The troll looked at the boy.

"Hey," shouted Skadi. "Focus on me."

Skadi leaped for the troll, sword held tightly in both hands, prepared to strike it down, but the monster caught the sword in its right hand and ripped the weapon away from her with such force that it shredded her palms.

The troll flung the sword over the cliff, then directed its attention once again towards Bjorn.

"Run," shouted Skadi.

She watched her boy pivot and take off in the opposite direction.

"Mom," he shouted as he reentered the forest from the cliffside clearing.

"I'm coming," yelled Skadi chasing after her son and the troll.

The troll's body was easy to follow as it barreled through smaller trees and dented larger ones. It lacked any grace, and Skadi could tell it was out of its element but did not know why. It was a mountain troll, and mountain trolls belonged in the mountains. Regardless, it was a massive creature and far stronger than her or Bjorn, and she had only a knife without her sword.

The creature stopped running, and for a second, Skadi feared it had caught Bjorn, but she saw it looking around. It must have lost sight of her son. She looked back and forth too but didn't see him. Then silhouetted against the partial moon, she saw the string of his bow being pulled back from up high in one of the trees.

"Do it," she whispered.

Her son let the arrow fly and exploded the troll's left eye. The creature grabbed its face crying out in pain, slamming its free hand into trees. One of the trees was where Bjorn had managed to scurry, and the force of the hit made him lose his balance. Skadi watched this happen in what felt like slow motion and ran to catch him. She reached him a second too late, and the boy's body hit the ground.

The troll wandered off, writhing in pain.

Skadi dropped to her son's side. He was breathing but just barely.

"No, no, no, no . . ." she kept repeating.

Skadi put her arms under the boy, lifted him off the ground, and carried him back to their campsite. Still alive and hitched to its post was Skadi's horse. She placed Bjorn on the horse and jumped up, so he was positioned under the reins in front of her.

"Yah," she said and squeezed with her upper calves so the horse would start galloping.

"Stay with me, son," she whispered as the horse carried them down the road.

"I . . . got . . . him," said Bjorn passing in and out of consciousness.

"You did," she said.

She squeezed her legs again to encourage the horse to go faster.

"If only Frija could have come with," whispered Skadi, thinking out loud. "Her magic could help, but Fensalir is too far away, and he won't survive a journey back. Even at this rate, we are still hours away from Hlíðarendi. Please hang on, son."

Skadi charged down the road as fast as her horse could muster while Bjorn's breathing steadied. Night became morning, and morning became midday. It was then that she saw smoke rising on the horizon. They were nearing the small town.

Bjorn coughed and spat up blood all over Skadi's right leg.

"Come on, you damn horse. Faster," she shouted.

Skadi jammed her heels into the horses' sides, and the dumb animal damn near killed itself, galloping as fast it could go to the gates of Hlíðarendi.

"Help," shouted Skadi as they approached. "My boy has been injured, and we need a healer now."

The gates parted, and a woman in a grey pelt came rushing out. She ushered the woman and child to a two-story cottage not far from the gate's entrance and helped Bjorn off the horse. She carried the child inside the cottage and cleared a table of debris before gently placing Bjorn down.

"What happened?" she said.

"Mountain troll," said Skadi.

"On the road?"

"Just off it."

"Curious," said the woman.

"How bad is he?" said Skadi.

The woman pulled back Bjorn's pelts, revealing a chest that was entirely black and blue. She gently touched the deepest shades.

"Broken ribs," she said. "I can treat him, but it'll be six weeks at least before he's sufficiently healed. During that time, I'm sure it's obvious that he can't travel for risk of further injuries."

"I understand," said Skadi.

"I can, however, speed up his recovery time for a price," she said.

"How?" Skadi said.

"Seidr magic," said the woman.

"Are you a witch?"

"I'm a Valkyrie. My name is Eir."

NINE

THE TASK

"Hlíðarendi is the home of Gunnar Hámundarson. He is a great hero and is highly revered in this town, but like all great heroes, his time is coming to an end. He was advised by a close friend not to kill two family members of Gissur the White, but he did, and men are on their way as we speak to exact their revenge. I can no longer perform the duties of the Valkyrie. It has taken its toll on me over the years, and I walk a different path now, but with Gunnar's death soon to happen in my town, I must oversee it. At least I did until you arrived. I can deputize you as temporary Valkyrie, and if you bear witness to Gunnar's death and see to it that he receives passage to Valhalla, I will heal your son immediately so you may continue on your journey," said Eir.

"All I have to do is oversee his death?"

"That's all," said Eir.

"I'll do it."

Eir grabbed Skadi's hand and placed in it a small amulet.

"When he is dead, do not be alarmed. He will appear beside you. Give him this so he may enter Valhalla. Go now. It's about to happen," said Eir.

"Where do I go?" said Skadi.

"Close your eyes."

Skadi did as instructed, and her world went black, save for the souls of the inhabitants of Hlíðarendi, but amongst them, one glowed a shade of red and brighter than the rest.

"See yourself there," said Eir.

Immediately Skadi felt like she fell through a well or a vacuum, and when she opened her eyes, she was standing in a room where multiple men were engaging in combat with a single fighter. Her appearance startled no one, and she quickly realized they could not see her.

Gunnar fought valiantly. He was extremely gifted, and if it were not for the overwhelming numbers he faced, he surely would win the day. In another life, Skadi would have loved to have sparred with him.

When it was all over, over two dozen men lay dead on the ground surrounding Gunnar, who was stumbling backward with a knife protruding from his stomach. As blood flowed from his abdomen, he lost his balance and caught himself on the edge of his bed. He leaned against the bedpost for a minute then fell to the ground.

Skadi bore witness to his death, then turned to her right and saw Gunnar standing next to her, staring at his still-warm corpse. For a second, not a word was said between them. Skadi wasn't even sure Gunnar was aware of her until he finally spoke.

"Are you a Valkyrie?" he said without facing her.

"I'm . . . yes," she said.

"You are here to take me to Valhalla?" he said.

"I am," said Skadi. "Well. To give you this."

She held up the amulet.

"I thought I'm to be escorted," said Gunnar.

"I'm sorry. I'm just supposed to give you this," she said.

"So much for the stories," he said.

Skadi didn't reply. Gunnar turned to face her.

"I've fought so many battles; it was only a matter of time until I was finally bested. One can only cheat death for so long before you have to play by the rules," said Gunnar. "I'll take the amulet."

"Was it worth it?" said Skadi.

"Was what worth it?" said Gunnar.

"Whatever it was that led to this?" she said.

"You only have one life, and no matter what, it will one day come to an end, and the best you can do is try and leave the world a better place than how you found it," said Gunnar. "Did I do that? I guess time will tell, but I know that Gissur the White and his family were bringing trouble to Midgard, and I stopped them."

Skadi handed Gunnar the amulet.

"You fought bravely," said Skadi.

Gunnar nodded.

"Each who takes up a weapon shall eventually die by it," he said and disappeared.

Skadi stood alone for a moment before closing her eyes and seeing herself once again by Eir and Bjorn. She opened her eyes, and there they were. Bjorn was lying on the table, and Eir stood over him, imparting a warm glow from her body to his.

"Thank you," said Eir.

"Mom," said Bjorn sitting up on the table.

She saw his exposed chest was no longer black and blue. Skadi walked over and hugged the boy.

"I was worried," she said.

"Gunnar was a fine warrior. Midgard is worst off without him," said Eir.

"I have seen few men fight harder and more skillfully," said Skadi. "He brought honor to himself and his home."

"Did you talk?" said Eir.

"Briefly," Skadi replied.

Eir patted Bjorn on the shoulder.

"You are good to go," she said.

He hopped off the table and felt his chest and upper abdomen. Bjorn took a deep breath and let it out slowly.

"I feel great. Better than even before the fall," he said.

"Come here, Skadi. Let me take care of your hands," said Eir.

Skadi stepped over to Eir and reached out her hands. That same warm glow that had been washing over Bjorn began flowing over Skadi, and she watched the wounds on her hands quickly heal.

"Was it your intention for me to speak with Gunnar?" said Skadi.

"He was wise and often gifted young warriors with pearls of wisdom. This journey you are on is no small feat. Frija thought it best you speak with him before he goes," said Eir.

"You know Frija?" said Skadi.

"She is a powerful ally to have, but she is confined to Fensalir. If she could make this journey, she would. The fact that she has entrusted it to you tells me a lot. I would have always healed your boy, but there was urgency with Gunnar," said Eir.

Eir released Skadi's fully healed hands.

"A mountain troll down from the mountain concerns me, though," said Eir. "I'm worried about what that might mean for the nine realms. Many creatures have been acting abnormally these past few months."

"Like a Valkyrie who refuses their duties?" said Skadi.

"Healing is part of deciding who lives and who dies," said Eir. "And so is teaching."

"Thank you," said Skadi.

"You are welcome. Now. I know you lost a horse in the battle with the troll. There is a stable in town where you can get a fine replacement and a blacksmith that forges powerful swords. Go prepare for the next stage of your journey," said Eir.

"Come, son," said Skadi.

"Thank you," Bjorn said to Eir.

At the stable, a man greeted them who called himself Hrimthur. He was tall and wide. His face wore a thick beard, and his eyes were pleasant and welcoming.

"Word is, you required a horse," said Hrimthur. "Let me show you what I have. The only horse finer than what's in my stable is ridden by Odin himself."

"We have little money," said Skadi.

"No need to concern yourself with that. Eir has helped me so much in life. This is a favor to her," he said.

"Bjorn, this horse is for you," said Skadi. "You decide."

Hrimthur showed him five different horses that ranged in age and height. Bjorn chose a robust, black steed, the same size as his mother's horse. Hrimthur outfitted the animal with a saddle and told them that they could take the horse with them when they were ready.

"My horses have been blessed by Eir and do not need rest and food like all others. They'll heal from nearly anything as well. Now that doesn't mean beat her up but just know she'll take care of you," said Hrimthur.

"Thank you," said Bjorn.

"You're welcome young man," said Hrimthur.

They proceeded to the forge from the stable, where a man dressed in black, and a face covered in soot greeted them. He introduced himself as Bo.

"Welcome," he said.

"We were sent by Eir," said Skadi.

"You'll find the finest weapons made by man here. I was taught how to forge weapons by a dwarf," Bo said.

"Who?" said Bjorn.

"Eitri himself," said Bo.

"Eitri?" said Bjorn in disbelief.

"The one and only maker of Thor's hammer," said Bo."

"That is impressive," said Skadi.

"I see the quiver around the boy, so I take it the close-quarter combat is left to you?" said Bo.

Skadi nodded.

"My previous sword was imbalanced," she said.

"Believe me when I say this . . . this one will not be. I must admit, though, that despite me having learned from dwarves, I'm still not a dwarf, so if you ever get the opportunity to trade up to a dwarven blade, do it," said Bo. "But until then, the sword I make you will slay any beast you find out there in Midgard."

"Thank you."

"Come back early tomorrow morning, and your weapon will be ready."

Skadi and Bjorn booked a room at an inn in town. They slept through the night. Skadi awoke first in the morning and saw her son still asleep, clutching a pendent his father had given him.

T E N

FATE

Skadi and Bjorn stood just inside the gates of Hlíðarendi with Eir, Hrimthur, and Bo. Morning dew still graced the ground. The sword Bo had forged was hitched to Skadi's side, and the horse Hrimthur had gifted Bjorn stood behind him.

Skadi observed the three strangers who became her and her son's friends in the span of 24 hours.

"May Heimdall watch over you on your journey," said Eir.

"Thank you all," said Skadi.

"Fensalir is a beautiful town," said Bo. "I've been a few times. This dark time it's facing doesn't define it, but it does need help."

"Farewell," said Hrimthur.

Skadi and Bjorn mounted their respective horses, waved goodbye, and exited through the front gate of Hlíðarendi.

The sun was still rising, and the morning was cool. The mother and son held their pelts close to their bodies to keep in the warmth. For a while, they trotted along the road towards Urðarbrunnr in quiet. The only sound was that of their horses' hooves touching the dirt road and the jingling of supplies they kept in their knapsacks.

They were another day's ride from the first location where they were to find the roots of Yggdrasill.

"How did you and father meet?" said Bjorn, breaking the silence.

"We met while traveling," said Skadi.

"So, you did not always know each other?"

"Yes," Skadi answered.

"Did you ever love anyone else?"

"No," said Skadi.

The conversation lulled, and the two traveled along the road for another hour in silence. The sun had burned away the morning dew, but the winter chill was ever present, and the mother and son duo could see their breath as they exhaled.

Midgardian winters usually lasted for half of the year. It made the nights long and the days short. It also served for a time of year when pillaging increased, encouraged by the need for supplies. It was this need that spurred ten men and women to start tracking Skadi and Bjorn as they traveled along the road away from Hlíðarendi towards Urðarbrunnr. This path took them further and further away from any semblance of civilization.

The ten men and women closed in as the road descended into a canyon, and the rocky walls shrouded Bjorn and Skadi in the shade.

A battle cry carried through the canyon.

"Bjorn, move ahead of me," said Skadi. "Now."

As instructed, he quickly positioned his horse ahead of hers.

"Fresh meat," shouted an unseen man.

"Bjorn, go," Skadi shouted.

Skadi observed her son squeeze his legs to encourage his horse, but a scraggy man wielding two blades dropped down in front of him. The horse neighed and reeled back on its hind legs. It kicked the man, sending him flying over the edge of the cliff face. He screamed until he hit the ground below.

An arrow zipped by Skadi's head. It ruffled her hair as it flew past her.

"Bjorn, keep moving," she shouted a second time.

He squeezed his horse again and shouted, "Yah."

His horse took off, and Skadi followed close behind.

Arrows rained down from the cliffs above, peppering the road behind them. The hooves of their horses galloped along, and the shouts of wild men and women filled the canyon.

"Who are they?" shouted Bjorn.

"Raiders," Skadi shouted back.

"We're hungry, and that boy looks well-fed," shouted a woman.

Skadi saw Bjorn look up and ready his bow. He fired as his horse followed the path they were traveling. The arrow connected with a feral-eyed woman, and she came tumbling over the cliff. She landed in front of Bjorn and Skadi. Their horses trampled what little life remained in her.

"This is our territory," shouted another unseen assailant.

Arrows continued to land at their horses' feet as they charged full speed ahead through the shaded canyon.

"Just keep riding as fast as you can," shouted Skadi as she watched Bjorn try returning fire as best as he could but failing to connect.

The canyon's exit was fast approaching, and Skadi and Bjorn would have greater freedom to combat their aggressors, but arrows were nipping at their backs. The cold was biting as the wind washed over their sweaty brows, and then just like that, they emerged into the open.

Eight riders on horseback were in hot pursuit of the mother and son. As far as hordes go, it wasn't the largest Skadi had ever seen. Far from it, in fact, but when considering she had to protect her son, they were a daunting foe.

The horde was collectively slower, and if their horses didn't give out, Skadi and Bjorn would outrun them. Then an arrow slammed into the neck of Skadi's horse.

When she came to, she quickly realized that they were surrounded. Bjorn was bravely standing over her with his bow drawn. She pulled herself to her feet and drew her blade.

"We'll kill you quick," said one of the men nearest them. "Ready your bows."

"Bjorn, I'm sorry," said Skadi.

"Wait," shouted one of the women in the horde.

A blonde-haired woman dressed in black pushed her way to the front.

"Skadi Hervor?" said the woman.

"Who knows me?"

"You may not remember me, but I remember you. Let them go," said the woman.

"Agata," said Skadi.

"So, you do remember?" said Agata.

"I do," said Skadi."

"You're a long way from home."

"We're on a journey."

"These men will not pursue you and your boy any further. But you know better than I to be careful out there. Midgard is not what it used to be, and it was never much," said Agata.

Skadi glanced at her horse, dead on the ground.

"Sorry about that," said Agata.

"Let's go," said Skadi to Bjorn.

"Is that the boy? Your child?" said Agata.

"That's him," said Skadi.

"He's a fine young man," said Agata. "He's very brave. Like your husband. Like you."

"Thank you," said Skadi.

She climbed atop his horse and pulled Bjorn up, so he sat behind her. Immediately they galloped off.

"Who was that woman?" asked Bjorn once they were out of view of the raiders that had just moments ago had them cornered.

"A long time ago, she needed help, and your father and I helped her. Thank Odin for her sense of honor."

"Honor? She is a Viking. They have no honor," said Bjorn.

"She remembered a debt and paid it. That is honorable."

"They were going to kill us."

"The rules of survival are different in Midgard the further you get from civilization. We are alive. Let us continue on our mission."

For hours, the mother and son rode in silence. Bjorn continuously looked back to see if anyone was pursuing them while Skadi kept her eyes forward.

The two came upon the location Frija had marked on the map as being Urðarbrunnr. It was the entrance to a cave at the edge of the forest. Skadi slid off the horse and walked up to the cave's mouth. She stood there for a moment, looking into the darkness.

"Hitch the horse," she said without turning around.

Skadi pulled a wooden stave from within her pelt and struck it with a piece of flint. A small fire formed at the tip of the stave, and Skadi held it over her head, lighting her immediate vicinity. Bjorn finished hitching the horse and appeared behind her.

"Perhaps you should stay with the horse," said Skadi.

"No," said Bjorn.

Skadi sighed.

"Stay close then," she said, taking her sword in her other hand.

The two descended into the cave, moving slowly and cautiously, the darkness held at bay by the fire Skadi wielded. They stopped momentarily when the entrance was no longer in sight.

Skadi observed her son, then nodded, and the two continued. Deeper they went, further and further underground. The cave was cold, damp, and disturbingly quiet. Their footsteps boomed, and the fire crackled. Both generated such great sound in the absolute quiet.

An hour into their journey underground, they came across an iron door.

An inscription across the top read "örlög."

"What does that mean?" said Bjorn.

"It means fate," said an icy voice from the other side of the passageway as the door opened, seemingly all on its own. "Welcome Skadi Hervor and Bjorn Hervor to Urðarbrunnr."

ELEVEN

THE JÖTUNN'S GIFT

The man who had left the inn reached Fensalir as the sun was peaking over the mountain. The rain had long since let up, though his pelt remained drenched, and his body was aching. He needed to rest. The journey had taken its toll on him, and despite his superior stamina and endurance, he was at his end.

"A bed," he said to the guard at the gate.

The guard hesitated, unsure whether to ask of this man's connection to Fensalir, but before saying anything, just pointed towards a small cottage with "INN" written on a sign out front. The man made for the building, booked a room, and crashed into the first bed he saw. He awoke that night, rejuvenated. The innkeeper heard him rummaging around and brought him some food.

He ate in silence before departing.

"So, this is where she's come," he whispered. "Quaint."

The man roamed around Fensalir, taking in its layout and its people. The residents of the town were mostly all inside their homes. He observed their actions through the windows, spying. One home appeared abandoned despite the building out back of it stocked with drying cod.

"Who is not home?" he whispered.

He made for the center of town and stopped at the council hall building. This was usually where town councils kept the log of their residents.

"And who is it you are looking for?" said the woman sitting at the desk right before the entrance to the council chambers within the council hall.

"Her name is Skadi Hervor," said the man.

"And your name, sir?"

"I'll take it from here," said Elfr Rói, who had just emerged from within the council chamber.

The man turned to face Elfr.

"Come with me," said Elfr.

The man looked back at the woman with whom he had just been speaking. She shrugged her shoulders and shifted her attention away from him.

"I'll explain in private," Elfr said.

The two men disappeared within the council chamber, and the woman put the registry of Fensalir's residents back under her desk.

"This town is so strange," she grumbled.

"Have a seat, Hovard," said Elfr once the door had closed.

"How do you know my name?" said Hovard.

"I know many things. I know that you're looking for Skadi and her son Bjorn. So are we," said Elfr.

"We?" Hovard said.

A door on the opposite side of the chamber creaked open, and a chill filled the room. The jötunn appeared, and Hovard leaped for his sword.

"What is going on here?" Hovard said.

Elfr raised a hand.

"Be calm. Neither of us are here to hurt you. We want to help you, and in return, you can help us," said Elfr.

Hovard eased his grip on his sword and let some of the tension out of his body. He remained on guard but at an eight rather than a ten.

"A witch has set Skadi and Bjorn on a collision course with us. It is a collision we think we can avoid with your assistance," said Elfr.

"What can I do?" said Hovard.

"Help me track them down. I know you have been looking for them for some time. Together we can find them," said Elfr.

"How do you know what I've been doing?" said Hovard.

"This jötunn can impart special gifts to those who accept them. He gave me the power to see inside people's heads but just the most recent thoughts. I can also control the minds of lesser beings. He is prepared to gift you with a power of your own but only if you help us with our cause," said Elfr.

"Do I get to choose the power?" said Hovard.

"It chooses you," said Elfr.

Hovard looked at the creature standing in the doorway.

"I know what drives you, Hovard. Let's make things right," said Elfr.

"I'm confident I don't need your help with Skadi," said Hovard.

"You will if she completes her journey. The power boosts she'll receive from the roots of Yggdrasill will put her on par with lesser Asgardians," said Elfr. "It won't matter how skillful of a warrior you are then. She will make quick work of you."

"Asgardians?" said Hovard. "Then why not just take the roots for myself? Why partner with a jötunn?"

"Because the World Tree does not respond to vengeance. What she will receive is not what you will," said the jötunn.

He walked across the room and stood before Hovard. The creature towered over him. He placed a hand on his shoulder and dug in with his claws. Hovard embraced the pain. He wouldn't let this beast know he was afraid.

"I know what it is like to be sworn off. To be betrayed. Take this gift and get your revenge," said the jötunn.

Hovard's body started to glow, and his eyes turned a burning red. A fire swirled at his feet that slowly engulfed him. It burned white-hot. Elfr turned away as not to be blinded.

"What is this?" shouted Hovard.

The jötunn released its grip, and Hovard took in a few deep breaths. The creature looked at Elfr and nodded, then disappeared from the room.

Hovard turned his palms skyward and formed small orbs of fire in them.

"This is the jötunn's gift," said Elfr. "I'm jealous, actually. That is an exciting power."

"What does this mean?" said Hovard.

"You have the power to get your revenge," said Elfr.

Hovard morphed the two fireballs into one large orb. He felt the warmth that it gave off but instinctually knew it would not hurt him. He increased its temperature so that it was white-hot, forcing Elfr to step back.

"Impressed?" said Elfr.

Hovard collapsed the fireball, returning the temperature of the room to just above what it was before.

"Very," he said.

THE NORNS

Skadi technically deflected, but the force of the impact sent her tumbling to the ground. Bjorn ran after his mother, but she shouted for him to stay where he was. He ignored her request and ran after her, but a powerful gust of wind lifted him off the ground and pushed him through the iron door from which they had come.

He pulled on the door, but it would not budge. Skadi was left alone on the other side.

"Mom," he shouted.

She pulled herself to her feet and wiped the blood and dirt from her face.

"Do you think you are deserving mortal?" said a ghostly figure that hovered over Skadi.

She pivoted and swung her sword at the creature. The blade cut through the creature but caused it no harm.

"What are you?" shouted Skadi.

The monster flew down and grabbed her by the pelt, and lifted her off the ground. It pulled her close so that its face and hers were only an inch apart.

"I see you for who you are," said the creature and threw her to the ground.

She caught herself breaking the impact, but it wasn't a pleasant landing. Skadi scraped her arm up bad and small rocks embedded in her skin.

Again, she got to her feet, and again she was thrown to the ground. This back and forth of her being thrown to the ground and her getting up happened until her bounce back was slower and slower. After the tenth time, Skadi had to use her sword to support her.

The ghostly figure positioned itself in front of her.

"You realize your efforts are futile," it said.

"And yet I persist," said Skadi.

"You are a fool," said the figure. "Do you know what I am?"

"Should I?"

"If you knew what we were, you would not have come," said the creature.

"We?" said Skadi.

Two other ghostly figures appeared alongside the one directly in front of her.

"We are the Norns," said the middle creature. "Now begone."

The same gust of wind that expelled Bjorn pushed Skadi through the passageway she had entered through and shut the iron door behind her.

"Mom," he said.

"I'm all right," she said. "It's all superficial."

"What is that thing?"

"There's three. They are the Norns. Their names are Urðr, Verðandi, and Skuld. I wasn't quite sure if they were real, but clearly," said Skadi looking at the wounds on her forearms, "they're real."

"What do we do?" said Bjorn.

"To go back in there and keep swinging away is foolish," said Skadi. "But I don't know how effective reasoning will be either. If my memory of their lore serves me correctly, these creatures determine the fates of all beings in the nine realms. Including the Asgardians and the Vanir. In some ways, they are above even the Allfather."

"Above the Allfather?" said Bjorn in disbelief.

"Why would Frija send us here? She had to know these creatures guarded the first root," said Skadi.

"Maybe she wanted us to meet them like how Eir wanted you to meet Gunnar?" said Bjorn.

"You should listen to the boy," said Urðr.

The iron door reopened. Skadi and Bjorn looked at it skeptically. Bjorn started for the door, but Skadi grabbed his arm.

"Behind me," she said.

She moved ahead of him, sword in hand, and cautiously reentered the cavern where moments ago she was being tossed around like a ragdoll.

"We commend your attempt, mortal," said Verðandi. "But even Odin seeks us out before doing something significant."

"In my defense," said Skadi. "You startled me."

There was a collective laugh among the three creatures; then, they appeared out of thin air. They hovered before Skadi and Bjorn, vaguely translucent. The stave Skadi had used to light their way through the cave was burning on the ground in the corner.

"Perhaps this should be a lesson to you not to strike first and ask questions later," said Skuld.

"As masters of fate, surely you knew we were coming," said Skadi.

"We did," said Urðr.

"Will we be successful in destroying the jötunn?" said Bjorn.

"We cannot say," said Verðandi.

"Why?" said Skadi.

"Because while Frija may have helped put you on the path, it is still up to you to walk it. If we told you that you would defeat the jötunn, you will likely make a foolish decision because you knew you would ultimately win the day. This would, of course, result in you failing. But if we did not tell you, you would continue to operate cautiously and make decisions that would win you the day. So, you see, we, like Frija, can help put you on the path to success, but we cannot say whether you will succeed," said Skuld.

"What now?" said Bjorn.

"Few in Midgard know this, but fate is a fluid thing. It changes, which you may think runs contrary to the whole idea of fate, but it does not. Fate is determined largely by past actions. We interpret those past actions to draw logical conclusions, and we are deadly precise. Skadi, your past actions do not bode well for your future," said Urðr.

"Will you give us the root?" said Skadi.

"Only if you answer a question correctly," said Verðandi.

"Let's have it," Skadi said.

"Why do you need it?" said Skuld.

"To defeat the jötunn," said Skadi. "Are you playing games?"

"Not at all, mortal. And that does not answer our question," said Urðr. "Why do *you* need the root?"

Skadi looked at her son. He, too, had a puzzled expression across his face.

"If you cannot answer this question, we cannot provide you with the root, and you must leave," said Verðandi.

"Wait," said Skadi.

"It should be obvious. If it is not, then you are not deserving, and Frija should have chosen a better champion," said Skuld.

"For him," said Skadi pointing at Bjorn. "I need the root so I can protect him. Fensalir is our home now, and I need to make it safe to raise my son."

"And is Bjorn the only child in Fensalir?" said Urðr.

"Of course not," said Skadi.

"And yet you only fight for him?" said Verðandi.

"I . . ." Skadi could not complete her thought.

"Do you see the flaw in your motivation?" said Skuld. "How could you ever be successful with such a myopic view? The root would be wasted on you. Go now."

"I can't leave without that root."

"And yet you will," said Urðr. "If it means anything, mortals are not the only being in the nine realms who think small. The gods are just as selfish."

"Wait a minute. I am fighting for everyone," said Skadi. "Just give me the root."

"You are a selfish person. Your desire to move to Fensalir was borne out of a desire only to protect your offspring, as was your desire to fight for Fensalir. Midgard does not need any more selfish people. As altruistic as it may seem to fight for the ones you love, you need to be able to fight for those you don't even know. Everyone needs help, but if we only focus on those close to us, Midgard does not improve," said Verðandi.

"I promise to fight for everyone if you give me the root," said Skadi.

"How can we trust you if you don't even trust your son with the truth?" said Skuld.

"The truth?" said Bjorn. "Mom, what is it talking about?"

"You are part of the problem, Skadi," said Skuld. "Your kind has been and will be a plague."

"Mom, your kind?" said Bjorn.

Skadi took a deep breath and turned around to face her son.

"I am a Viking, Bjorn. Your father was a Viking. But the Viking age has long ended. Those raiders you claim are Vikings are just violent men and women who bastardize a way of life that no longer exists. I became one of them too, but your father and I left that life and chose to live as nomads when you were born. The woman you met earlier, Agata, was a friend from a past life long ago," said Skadi.

Bjorn looked at the ground and dug his foot into the dirt.

"I was going to tell you."

Bjorn looked up at the Norns then back at the ground.

"That is not who I am anymore," said Skadi.

"Who are you then?" Bjorn said without looking up at her.

"I am your mother."

He glanced up at her.

"Does that make me a Viking or a raider . . . whatever you call your-selves?" said Bjorn.

"You are what you choose to be. What your father and I were, is not what you have to be. You can be better than both of us, son," said Skadi.

"But I don't want to be better than dad . . . just you."

Skadi took a deep breath in through her nostrils and let out a long sigh. She nodded and turned away from her son.

A shining light glowed, drawing the attention of Skadi and Bjorn. They looked towards it, and the three Norns were standing before them in the form of three women dressed in white. Urðr's hand was outstretched and in it was the source of the light.

"For both of you," said Urðr.

Skadi grabbed the Yggdrasil root and split it in half, keeping a piece for herself and handing the other half to Bjorn. They observed the glow-ing root, then took a leap of faith and consumed it. For a second, there was nothing. They even began to wonder if it did anything then each felt their bodies start to tremble. A tingling sensation flowed from the bottom of their feet up through the top of their heads. Their fingertips glowed, and arcs of electricity leaped from their bodies, connecting with the walls of the cave.

"Mom?" said Bjorn.

The walls and floor of the cave started shaking. Stalactites fell from the ceiling, crashing around Skadi and Bjorn. The arcs of electricity increased in size and became more frequent, lighting up the cave like a storm, then a burst of energy erupted from within the two. It exploded at the entrance of the cave knocking over a few small trees nearby.

Skadi and Bjorn blacked out for a moment, and when they came to, they were on all fours on the floor of the cave. A few arcs of electricity still danced around the cave before dissipating. Skadi used her sword to stand up then assisted her son in getting to his feet.

The wounds she had received attempting to fight the Norns were gone, and the muscular mass throughout her entire body had increased. Bjorn, too, looked stronger and slightly older, as though his body had aged to compensate for the increase in strength.

Skadi picked up a rock roughly the size of a human head. With a strong clench of her fist, she turned it into pebbles.

"We wish you success on your journey," said Verðandi.

"But be warned that the jötunn you seek to slay is not like the other beasts of the nine realms. If you manage to kill it, you will be provoking the gods," said Skuld.

Before Skadi or Bjorn could ask how they would be provoking the gods, the Norns disappeared, and all that remained were the boy and his mother.

TO VALHALLA

Elfr and Hovard approached the town of Hlíðarendi, and Eir greeted them at the gate. She sensed the men's intent but asked of their purpose for visiting anyway.

"We are searching for a woman and her child," said Elfr. "We believe she may have passed through this town."

"What did this woman look like?" said Eir feigning ignorance.

"Do not play coy, Valkyrie. We know she was here. How long ago did she move on? We just need to gauge how much of an advantage she has on us," said Elfr.

"There was no woman," said Eir.

"One day," said Elfr, having read Eir's mind.

"How did you . . ." asked Eir.

"The question made you consider the answer even if you didn't verbalize it. I have a gift," said Elfr.

Eir drew an inquisitive look upon her face and glanced at Hovard, who remained quiet during the question-and-answer parring.

"If we head straight to Hvergelmir, we can cut them off. They'll have already acquired the first root, but it won't matter," said Elfr to Hovard.

"Wait a minute now," said Eir. "You two aren't going anywhere before you answer some questions."

"Let's ride," said Elfr to Hovard, ignoring Eir.

"Stop," shouted Eir.

A bolt of lightning struck the ground where she was standing and when it was gone, her clothing had changed to an armor-plated pelt. In her left hand was a shield, and in her right hand a sword. Wings sprouted from her back that spanned twelve feet. This transformation garnered the attention of Elfr and Hovard.

"I think you're up," said Elfr to Hovard.

Hrimthur and Bo positioned themselves in the guard posts of the gate to see what was happening.

"I thought she swore off her ways," said Bo.

"There must be something in Skadi and Bjorn that she sees worth fighting for," said Hrimthur.

Hovard dropped from his horse, his eyes glowing red.

"Human, I don't care what that jötunn has done; you cannot stand against a Valkyrie," said Eir.

A warmth emanated from Hovard, and then a noticeable glow. His horse whinnied and backed up. Elfr followed suit, leaving Hovard and Eir facing off against one another at the gates of Hlíðarendi.

"I'll give you one last chance to turn around," said Eir. "If you don't take it, I will make sure you see Hel."

"A test of strength is necessary to know you've achieved new heights," said Hovard.

"Very well," said Eir.

A powerful flap of her wings propelled her forward; her sword pointed for a strike. Flames erupted around Hovard, and he dodged left. Eir caught the ground, turned, and swept for his head. He ducked the strike and put a well-placed fireball in her abdomen. The blow sent her tumbling through the dirt.

Eir got to her feet and patted the flames burning on her armor. Concern was creeping into her head, but she wouldn't let Hovard see it. She positioned herself in a fighting stance and prepared to go again.

Eir and Hovard exchanged blows so fierce that Elfr had to position himself hundreds of feet from the battlefield. Eir and Hovard were fearsome warriors, neither willing to give an inch, but there was a superior aggressor. An unwillingness to give ground did not mean she didn't.

Hovard was faster, and the flames that he emitted burned so hot that not even the legendary armor of the Valkyrie was effective at keeping it at bay. The fight wasn't one-sided yet, but if it persisted for too much longer, Hovard would undoubtedly come out on top.

"You saw that? That is not good," said Hrimthur and Bo in unison, observing the fight.

"We need to help her," said Bo.

"What can we do?" said Hrimthur.

"I have a weapon in my forge that I've been working on for the day Eir decided she wanted to be a Valkyrie again. But it isn't finished. It's a two-man job. If we move quickly, we can finish it and give it to her," said Bo.

"Then let's be quick about it," said Hrimthur.

The two men ran to the forge. Even out of sight, they could feel the battle happening just outside the gates of their town. The fight would be over soon if they did not help. They quickly reached the forge and got to work.

"Get the fire burning," shouted Bo, directing Hrimthur to the large hearth in the center of his cottage.

Bo disappeared into the basement of the cottage and came back up moments later, carrying a block of metal covered in a cloth with runic symbols on it.

"Eitri gave me this when I finished studying under him. It's Dwarven metal. It's impossible to forge unless you have help because as it heats up, the magic that blesses it causes it to get heavier and heavier unless there is a second person there to help carry the load. This is why Eitri always forged with his brother Brokkr," said Bo. "Here, take one handle of the tong."

Hrimthur did as he was instructed. Bo pulled the rune-covered cloth off the piece of metal and took the other handle of the tong. The two men inserted the Dwarven metal into the forge and waited until it started glowing.

Eir bounced off the gate of Hlíðarendi, cracking the wooden structure. She fell to the ground, bloodied and burned. She was perplexed—this human enhanced as he may have been should not be besting her like this. She slammed her fist into the ground in frustration, cracking the ground and exploding dirt into the sky.

"You fight for someone who you hardly know against someone who you do not, and you are losing. Are you a fool, Valkyrie?" said Hovard standing over her.

"I'm fighting for someone I believe in," replied Eir. "Against someone who means to harm innocents. The fool is the person who takes power from a jötunn and thinks it won't end in catastrophe."

Hovard placed one foot on the back of Eir, pushing her face in the dirt. He grabbed her wings and pulled. He lit up his hands in flames, burning her where he held them. The pain was piercing, and Eir let out a deep cry.

"He's killing her," shouted Hrimthur.

"It's finished," said Bo pulling the newly forged sword from the slack tub.

"Give it to me. I'll get it there quicker," said Hrimthur.

He whistled, and seconds later, a powerful, black steed appeared out front of Bo's forge.

"The sword is called Dáinsleif. It will not fail in its stroke. The wounds it will cause won't heal," said Bo.

Hrimthur mounted his horse.

"Be careful," said Bo.

"Yah," shouted Hrimthur, and he took off with Dáinsleif in hand.

Elfr standing back from the battlefield, witnessed the gates of Hlíðar-endi open, and Hrimthur come riding out with a giant sword, gleaming in the sun.

"Hmph," he said as he scanned the man's mind. "Oh no, you don't."

Elfr used his power to manipulate the minds of beasts to take control of Hrimthur's horse, and the creature turned away from Eir and back towards the gate entrance. Hrimthur recognizing quickly he had lost control and leaped from the horse and tumbled to a stop in the dirt.

"Hovard, don't let him get the sword to the Valkyrie," shouted Elfr.

Eir looked left and saw Hrimthur getting to his feet. A burst of strength surged within her, and she threw Hovard from her back. The ground under her crumbled as she emitted a golden glow. Eir rose, her eyes striking and focused, fire raging within her. She flapped her wings and blasted off into the sky.

Hovard tracked her movements and put his palms up, preparing to shoot her down but as quick as he had her in his sights, she disappeared with the sun to her back. She reappeared without time for him to react and placed a powerful kick to his chest, sending him flying. He hit the ground with a thud.

"Shit," said Elfr.

"Throw the sword," shouted Eir.

"Right," whispered Hrimthur.

He mustered what strength he could and threw the sword, knowing he would not reach her on foot before Hovard recovered from the last exchange. Eir flapped her wings to propel herself towards the sword, and just as the weapon's handle was about to meet her hand, the blade entered the side of Hrimthur's horse. It fell over dead immediately, and flames washed over Eir, blasting her back, scorching her entire body.

Hovard was up, and he came running at her, keeping up the attack. Wave after wave of fire washed over her. The feathers of her wings erupted in flames and burned away. Her armor melted in places, and the pelt itself blackened.

"Finish her," shouted Elfr.

Hovard increased the flames that emanated from his body and washed over hers. Eir fell to one knee, and Hovard let up on the attack. When the smoke cleared, she was barely alive. Her exposed skin blackened, and the armor she wore fused into a molten mass. Her wings were nearly nonexistent.

Bo and Hrimthur saw what had become of Eir, and dread swept over them both.

"Odin, please help her," whispered Bo.

"Valkyrie, I want you to know that you fought valiantly, and you have my respect. I never faced such a foe, and I doubt I ever will again," said Hovard.

"You're . . . a . . . monster," said Eir coughing up blood.

"I am driven by purpose as you once were, I'm sure. If that makes me a monster, then so be it. But neither you or anyone will stand in my way," said Hovard turning to look back at Hrimthur and Bo.

"Please . . . spare them," said Eir.

Hovard nodded.

"They are not a threat as long as they cease their intrusion. You have my word," said Hovard.

Eir watched Hovard raise his right palm. It started to glow. She mustered what remained and got to her feet.

"Valhalla awaits you," said Hovard.

A white glow blanketed the battlefield, and when it dissipated, only Hovard remained.

"No," shouted Bo.

Hovard immediately turned around and saw Elfr cut down Hrimthur with Dáinsleif. Bo started to retreat within the gate.

"Stop," shouted Hovard. "I gave her my word."

"They'll only come after us. The blacksmith is too dangerous to let live," said Elfr.

Elfr launched the sword into the air. Hovard targeted the newly forged weapon with a wave of fire but missed, and the sword made from Dwarven metal stabbed through the back of Bo, pinning him to the gate of Hlíðarendi.

"You should not have done that," said Hovard, flames swirling around his feet.

"We are on the same side. We want the same thing," said Elfr.

"They were defenseless," said Hovard.

"I know you want to kill me now, but in time you'll see that I am right," said Elfr.

"Or that you are a coward," said Hovard.

"Let's go," said Elfr.

"Lo, there do I see the line of my people back to the beginning. Lo, they do call to me, they bid me take my place among them in the halls of Valhalla, where thine enemies have been vanquished, where the brave shall live forever," whispered Hovard.

Elfr walked over to Bo and pulled the sword from his back.

"The jötunn made Hovard more powerful than I thought. Better hold onto this just in case," he whispered.

He looked at Hovard, who was standing over the scorched earth where Eir had stood.

"Surface thoughts have never painted a complete picture of a person, but maybe there is even more to this man than I considered," whispered Elfr.

FOURTEEN

A QUORUM IS NEEDED

Skadi and Bjorn emerged from the cave of the three Norns moments after consuming the first of the Yggdrasil roots they had sought after. The power of the World Tree had transformed her and Bjorn's bodies. She could feel how they were physically superior to their past selves in every way.

She watched Bjorn test his newfound strength by leaping in one bound to the top of the nearest tree, catching on to the highest branch, hanging there for a moment, then dropping to the ground without any show of pain in his legs and joints. She tested her newfound strength by cutting down a tree in a single strike.

"I can't believe it worked," said Skadi watching the tree topple to its side. "The root of the Yggdrasil really made us stronger."

Skadi saw Bjorn feel his arms and his legs.

"They no longer have any give. They're pure muscle," he said. "I feel invincible. Is that how you felt as a Viking or as a raider?"

"No," said Skadi.

"I can't imagine you feeling any different. Everyone was . . . is still afraid of Vikings," said Bjorn.

"People respected Vikings and fear raiders, and they have good reason for both, but neither are invincible, and we never felt that way," said Skadi.

"Mom, why do you intend to make a clear distinction between Vikings and raiders? I've heard from others what Vikings have done . . .

it isn't all just harmless exploration. Are Vikings bad, or are they good?" said Bjorn.

"That's a complicated question," Skadi said.

"What about dad? Was he good or bad? What was he like before me?" said Bjorn.

"He was merciful, and he was always kind."

"How could he be a Viking then?"

"To indulge one's savagery is easy. Especially in Midgard. But he regularly exercised restraint," said Skadi. "Sometimes to his own detriment."

"What about you?" said Bjorn.

Skadi looked at her boy, who now resembled more of a young man. He had looked his age of ten years before consuming the root but now look like someone in their early teens. Their eyes met.

"I was not your father," she said.

"What does that mean?" said Bjorn.

"Hvergelmir is a two-day ride, and we are down to one horse. We need to get moving," said Skadi.

She mounted the horse and reached out for Bjorn. He looked at his mom and hesitated.

"Come, son," she said.

He grabbed her hand and positioned himself behind her. Skadi squeezed her legs, and the horse took off.

In Fensalir, Dana Robert, Liótr Goti, and Lofn Lamont sat around the massive oak table in the council chamber.

"The jötunn chose our town because no one cares about it. The people here are poor, and there are limited natural resources to be scoured. But if Frija is sending warriors out into Midgard with the hope of drawing attention to Fensalir's plight, we are going to soon have a serious problem on our hands," said Dana.

"What are you suggesting?" said Liótr.

"Elfr and that newcomer are tracking down Skadi and her boy. But that won't mean much if we don't do something about Frija," said Dana.

"She is a powerful witch," said Lofn. "We've let her be, and she's treated us the same."

"That has clearly changed, and we need to respond," said Dana.

"What do you propose?" said Liótr.

"Someone trapped her in Fensalir with powerful Seidr magic, and even though she is a powerful practitioner of the same magic, she can't seem to break her bondage," said Dana.

"We are aware of this," said Lofn.

"Frija's cottage is at the edge of town. We should vote to redraw the lines of Fensalir, so her cottage falls outside of them," said Dana.

"And that will do what?" said Liótr.

"Frija stores most of her runes and spells in her cottage," said Dana.

"And if her cottage falls outside of Fensalir, the spell that keeps her here will also keep her from her runes," said Lofn.

"Then we kill her," said Dana.

"Without Petronilla and Elfr, we do not have a quorum. Even if we wanted to vote on this, we couldn't," said Liótr.

"We recruit someone to take Petronilla's place," said Dana.

"Who?" said Lofn.

"Someone grieving who would believe that the only witch in Fensalir could have something to do with the death of their child," said Dana.

Buna and Alver were sitting down to dinner when a knock at their door drew their attention away from their meal.

"Who is it?" said Buna.

"Ma'am, it's councilwoman Dana Robert. I'm here with Liótr Goti and Lofn Lamont. They're both council members as well. Do you have a moment to talk?" said Dana.

Buna looked at her husband questionably. He shrugged his shoulders. Buna got up and opened the door just as Dana was about to speak again.

"Yes?" said Buna.

"Ma'am, we are so sorry to bother you at this late hour. We know you are having dinner, but there is an urgent matter we'd like to discuss with you and your husband," said Dana.

"What is it?" said Buna.

"Can we come inside?" said Dana.

Buna stepped out of the way and gestured for the three council members to enter. Alver was still sitting at the table.

"Please have a seat," said Dana.

The three council members did as instructed.

"Ma'am, sir, we'll get right to it. Recently one of our council members was killed. I'm not sure how closely you follow Fensalir politics, but her name was Petronilla Wilde," said Dana.

"I follow. We both do. We're sorry for your loss," said Buna.

"Thank you. She'll be missed dearly," said Dana. "The reason we are here is that her seat is not up for reelection for another two years and our laws dictate that in the event of death or resignation, we can appoint a replacement to finish the term."

"And you want one of us to step up? Is that why you're here?" said Buna.

"You specifically. No offense, sir," said Dana.

"I would have told you no," said Alver.

"What do you say, Buna? Would you be willing to fill the remainder of Petronilla's term?" said Dana.

"Why me?" said Buna.

"We know you recently lost a son, and you've been very vocal about our inability to find his killer or the killer of the other children here in Fensalir. But we have reason to believe it is a woman named Frija who lives at the edge of town," said Dana.

"If you have a suspect, why not apprehend her?" said Buna.

"Because Frija is a witch. A powerful witch who is trapped in Fensalir by even more powerful seidr magic. If we were to apprehend her now, we would be dooming anyone we sent after her. But if we can vote her home out of Fensalir, where she stores most of her runes, we will hopefully take her peacefully. We need a quorum to make that vote. We need you," said Dana.

A mix of curiosity and concern spread across Buna's face. She turned to look at her husband.

"Can you give us a moment?" she said.

"Of course," said Dana.

Buna gestured for Alver to follow her into the bedroom, and he did.

"Do you think this is real?" she whispered.

"Sounds real, I think," he said.

"A witch in Fensalir?" said Buna.

"Do you remember the fuss over the rune fee? They said the runes protecting this town were waning in power," said Alver.

"So?" said Buna.

"So maybe there was some truth to that," said Alver.

"Are you saying I should do this then?" said Buna.

"You'll be in the public eye, and it seems the first vote they'll expect you to take is going to be controversial, but if it means bringing an end to the killings, then yeah, I think you should do it," said Alver.

"Okay. You're right," said Buna. "I'll do it."

Dana, Liótr, and Lofn were sitting, talking amongst themselves. They shifted their gaze towards Buna and Alver when the couple emerged from the bedroom.

"Can we count on you?" said Dana.

"You can," said Buna.

"Wonderful. This is the start of a new story for Fensalir," Dana said. "Let's head back to the Council Hall. The sooner we get this done, the better."

Frija held onto a seeing-rune and closed her eyes. Right away, a bird's eye view of Skadi and Bjorn appeared before her. They were riding along on horseback. Bjorn was holding onto Skadi.

"What happened to their other horse?" she whispered.

The ground beneath her feet shook, and she dropped the seeing-rune. It bounced off her foot and rolled under the stove. The vision of Skadi and Bjorn faded.

"What is going on?" Frija whispered.

The ground shook violently, rocking the house then the front door flew open. A powerful wind washed over Frija. It tugged at her with greater and greater ferocity, then lifted her off her seat. Shelves flew open, and their contents were strewn across the dining room.

Frija grabbed the chair to anchor herself, but whatever was tugging at her increased in force at a commensurate rate. She lost her grip, and her body flew across the room towards the open front door. She caught the door frame, stalling the inevitable, but a final push knocked her free, and she tumbled through the dirt in the shadow of her cottage.

Frija picked herself up and patted the dirt from her face. She walked back to her cottage, but as she got closer, an invisible force acted on her that kept her from reaching the front door. It was at that moment that she knew what had happened.

"Clever," she whispered.

Frija pulled out a rune from her pocket. It lit up as she brought it close to her face.

"Eir," she spoke into the rune.

Frija waited for a response, but none came.

"Eir," she repeated.

Still, there was nothing.

"Skadi," she said.

There was a moment of quiet and then a response.

"How are you speaking to me?" said Skadi.

"Magic. That's not important. What is important is this: the council members have redrawn the lines of Fensalir not to include my home. I've been cut off from most of my most powerful magic runes, so they'll be coming for me shortly. Have you and Bjorn made it to Urðarbrunnr?"

"They redrew the lines?" said Skadi.

"I'm confined to Fensalir, and the council members know this. They shrank the size of the town to cut me off from my most powerful tools. Before anything happens to me, I need to know you two are doing well on your journey," said Frija.

"We've consumed the first of the Yggdrasil roots and are on our way to Hvergelmir now," said Skadi. "If something happens to you, should we expect anything when we return to Fensalir?"

"No. The jötunn will surely try and access my magic, but it won't break my spells. It'll have no success with it."

"Okay," said Skadi.

"Did you stop in Hlíðarendi?" said Frija.

"We did."

"Was Eir helpful?" said Frija.

"She was," Skadi replied. "Look, Frija, take care of yourself. We will be back as soon as possible."

"I know you will. Someone is coming. If we don't speak again, thank you," said Frija.

Frija severed the communication with Skadi and ducked behind a large bush. Voices were approaching.

Liótr was with three men. Each wielded a sword and shield.

"Fan out," said Liótr. "She is around here somewhere."

Without the runes she kept stored in her home and having long been cut off from her true source of power, Frija was severely disadvantaged until she had time to rebuild her stockpile of runes, but that would take months she did not have. She listened as the men moved about, plotting an escape. There was enough shrubbery to keep her covered for a while, but there was an opening in that covering that she would not be able to avoid.

"You two gather whatever you can carry from her home. We'll be back for the rest later. You come with me," said Liótr directing the three men.

Frija spied the two men enter her cottage, and Liótr and the third man started towards the opening in the shrubbery. Next to her was a large rock. She picked it up and held it over her head, ready to strike.

Liótr and the man reached the opening and stopped. Frija was just out of their line of sight, but any further and they would see her. Sweat beads formed on her brow.

"Not another step," she whispered.

"Sir," said one of the men standing in the doorway of the cottage. "We found something you may want to take a look at."

"What is it?" said Liótr.

"I think you should see it for yourself," said the man.

"You stay here," said Liótr and went to meet the two men in the cottage home.

Frija followed Liótr with her eyes until he disappeared inside her home. She then switched her attention back to the man standing just around the corner from her.

"Now's my chance," she whispered.

"What am I looking at?" said Liótr when he met his two men.
One man held up a cloth. Liótr gave him a confused look.
"Sir, this is a swaddling blanket," said the man.
"And?" said Liótr.
"Look whose name is on it."
Liótr took the blanket and held it up.
"Oh," he whispered.
A yell caught the attention of Liótr and his two men inside the cottage. They all rushed outside and saw the third man lying on the ground, unconscious.
"Shit," shouted Liótr.

Frija put as much distance as she could manage between her and the four men at her home. A dangerous game of cat and mouse had just begun. She was not the cat.

THE BEAST

Skadi and Bjorn arrived at the base of a mountain which, as indicated by Frija's map, was Hvergelmir. The mountain was massive. Its peak was shrouded in clouds.

"The Yggdrasil root is at the top?" said Bjorn.

"I suppose it is," replied Skadi.

She steered the horse towards the start of the climb, but the creature reared, nearly unseating Skadi and Bjorn.

"Easy girl. What is it?" said Skadi.

A violent roar originating at the peak of the mountain carried across the land. Skadi and Bjorn looked up but did not see anything.

"What was that?" said Bjorn.

"Get off," said Skadi and directed Bjorn to step down from the horse.

"No. I want to help," he said.

"You can help by staying here."

"Mom, I can help. I'm just as strong as you are."

"But your life has more value," she said.

A second roar descended upon them.

"Get off the horse," shouted Skadi.

"Mom, I am with you on this journey," said Bjorn.

Skadi hesitated. She let out a deep sigh, then relented.

"Just promise me that if I say run, you will run," she said.

"I promise."

Skadi again tried to get the horse to climb, but again she reared.

"We'll have to do this on foot," she said.

Skadi hitched the horse to a stake, and the two began the long trek up the mountain.

"When you said that you were not dad, what did you mean?" said Bjorn.

"I did not share his knack for forgiveness, but I am working on that."

A few hours into their ascent, they reached a fallen tree, splintered in a manner that made it seemed as if someone knocked it over rather than chopped it down or uprooted it.

"What could have done this?" said Bjorn.

While Bjorn inspected the splintered base, it was the scorched branches that caught Skadi's attention.

"Stay on guard," she said.

The two climbed over the fallen tree and continued their journey. Another few hours into their ascent, a horrendous odor wafted across their nostrils.

"What is that?" said Bjorn.

"Sulfur."

The peak was fast approaching. Skadi noticed something and unsheathed her sword to face it. A massive snake slithered across their path. It paid them no mind and went over the edge of the walkway down the mountain.

There was the roar again. It bellowed, louder now.

"We are close. Let's go," she said.

"Mom, watch out."

She stopped mid-step. Crossing in front of her were dozens of snakes varying in size and species. Skadi recoiled to get proper footing.

"What is this?" she whispered.

They moved like a wriggling stream. Some hissed at her and Bjorn, but they mostly ignored their presence. It went on like this for some time, the last straggler finally going over the edge ten minutes after the first one appeared.

"That was odd," said Bjorn.

Skadi checked and didn't see any more.

"I think we can continue," she said.

They moved beyond where the snakes had crossed. Skadi looked back and saw Bjorn follow the swarm with his eyes as they moved down the mountainside. She saw him shiver before he caught up to her.

The mother and son hit a few switchbacks on the trail, then an open expanse devoid of trees, and looked out over Midgard. The two stood there for a moment, briefly taking in the view. In the distance, they could see Himinbjorg Mountain that overlooked Fensalir. Comparatively, the peak of Himinbjorg towered over the peak of the Hvergelmir, but that did not make their current hike seem any less strenuous.

A third roar shook the pair from their moment of solitude. It sounded as if it were right behind them. The smell of sulfur was at its strongest now. Bjorn pinched his nose.

"I know what is up there. It's a fearsome creature that no mortal has ever stood against," said Skadi.

"What is it, mom?" he said.

A gust of wind ripped across the area where they stood. They braced themselves against it, but the force was so powerful that they slid backward a foot. The clouds parted and hovering over them, its wings outstretched, was . . .

"A dragon," said Bjorn in horrified astonishment.

The beast parted its mouth, and from it came a river of fire. Skadi tackled Bjorn out of the way. They tumbled over the side of the mountain, rolling over bushes and snapping twigs under their combined weight. When they finally stopped, the two picked themselves up and looked back to the place from where they had fallen. Through the trees, they saw the dragon and fires raging.

"Mom, your sword," said Bjorn.

It was lying one hundred feet away, just below the dragon.

"You said a human has never survived a dragon," said Bjorn.

"I did say that," said Skadi.

"Then what are we going to do?" said Bjorn.

"We're going to fight," Skadi said.

"But mom—"

"We do not have a choice," said Skadi. "But I am going to need my sword."

The dragon flapped its wings and left its perch atop the mountain. It flew in a circle, engulfing the surrounding tree line in flames. The creature's roar was piercing—almost horrifying.

"Stay close," said Skadi. "And get your bow ready."

Bjorn did as instructed and pulled an arrow from his quiver. Skadi led him back up the side of the mountain. They did not follow the clear-cut path this time but rather the steep incline they had tumbled down. Their bodies ached, and both had scratches up and down their legs and arms, but they persisted even as the heat of the dragon's flames grew unbearable.

The sword was nearly in reach, but a gust of wind alerted Skadi and Bjorn to the dragon's approach. They leaped away from the weapon just in time to avoid another wave of fire. It washed over the sword and left the ground around it in flames.

"Shit," said Skadi in frustration.

They ducked below the ridgeline.

"We need a strategy," said Bjorn.

"We need to distract it. Give me your bow and quiver," said Skadi.

Bjorn did as he was told.

"Do you see that ridge up there?" said Skadi pointing at a plane higher than where they were.

"I do," he said.

"I'm going to snake my way around until I get there. When you see me, wait until I get the dragon's attention. When I have it, run and grab my sword. Can you do that?" said Skadi.

"I can," Bjorn replied.

Skadi grabbed the back of Bjorn's head and looked him in the eyes. She nodded, then departed.

He ducked down and waited as the dragon flew overhead. It continued to roar and blow fire in all directions, lighting up the sky with its flames. But as soon he saw his mother appear on the ridge she had pointed to, he perked up. She was crawling to minimize her visibility, but Bjorn noticed her, and soon so would the dragon.

"This is it," he whispered.

Bjorn saw his mother get on one knee and take an arrow in her hand. The dragon passed overhead, and she pulled the arrow back in the bow. She traced the sky, tracking the dragon's movement. He could see her preparing for her shot. She had closed one eye, and then she let the arrow fly. It raced through the sky faster than any arrow had ever flown before and pierced the dragon's neck. The creature let out a fearsome cry and turned its attention toward her.

Bjorn jumped to his feet and ran into the open.

Skadi let go of another arrow, and it too punctured the flesh of the enraged dragon. The beast opened its mouth, and Skadi could see the glow coming from within the dragon's throat. She let another arrow fly, but as it cut through the air, the wave of fire that burst forth from the dragon's mouth incinerated it.

The flame descended upon Skadi, but she quickly evaded incineration herself by leaping over the edge of the ridge. The dragon turned to go after her and, in doing so, noticed Bjorn running across the open plain towards the sword.

"No, you don't," said Skadi and jumped from her perch, catching the tail of the dragon firmly in her grasp.

The dragon shifted its attention away from Bjorn and now aimed to free itself from the stowaway that had latched herself to its being. It tried to shake her free, but her newfound strength was immense, and she dug in deep. The dragon turned upward and quickly darted towards the upper limits of Midgard's atmosphere.

Skadi clawed her way up the back of the beast as wind raced over her. It was difficult to breathe, and her pelt flapped violently. From her vantage point, Skadi saw Bjorn grab the sword but was now too high to drop free. She was midway between the dragon's tail and its head, and the dragon was still ascending. The mountain's peak was starting to shrink in the distance, and Skadi wondered momentarily if any human had ever been so high. She continued to make her way towards the creature's head.

The beast spun around, and Skadi briefly lost her footing, but her grip was so firm she nearly peeled back a scale to hold on. Skadi grabbed scale after scale and eventually moved onto the dragon's neck. The dragon roared and spewed fire from its mouth. When it did this, Skadi could feel the warmth pass through its neck.

Bjorn had struggled to carry the sword since it was burning hot from the dragon's flames. He threw the blade to the ground and began covering it in the dirt to extract the heat from the handle when he stopped mid-task.

"The root is unguarded," he whispered.

Bjorn left the sword where it lay and spied a well at the very peak of the mountain, which was positioned just over the ridge where his mother had perched to create the distraction.

"That's it," he said.

Bjorn crawled to the perch his mom had been standing on and looked up. The well was just overhead. Upon reaching it, he peered inside and caught a glimpse of something glowing beneath the surface of the water. He stuck his hand in the water and rummaged around until he grabbed it.

The dragon turned around mid-flight and began an accelerated descent. Faster than it rose, it raced towards the mountain. Skadi powered forward, and as the mountain returned into focus, she reached the dragon's head.

The creature's neck warmed under Skadi, and she knew the dragon was about to unleash a blast of fire. She pulled an arrow from the quiver, and just as the beast opened its mouth, she stabbed the arrow deep into the creature's left eye. The monster roared violently, and the fire it meant for Bjorn spewed right, missing him entirely. The beast flung Skadi from its back, and she went crashing into the side of the mountain just below Bjorn's location.

"Mom," shouted Bjorn.

He jumped down to where she laid and found her bloodied and broken, barely clinging to life.

"Mom here," he said, holding out the glowing Yggdrasil root he'd taken from the well.

But she wouldn't grab it. The dragon screeched. Bjorn looked up and saw the beast turning in the sky for a second pass. He had to act quickly. Bjorn broke the root in half and consumed his part. Just as before, power surged through his veins.

"Mom, I need you to eat this," he said, turning back to his mother and holding her half of the root to her lips.

She attempted to raise her hand but couldn't grab the root, and the dragon was fast approaching.

"I'll buy you some time," said Bjorn.

He placed the root in his mother's hand, grabbed the quiver and bow, and leaped from the ridge. He put two arrows in the bow at once, pulled back further than he had ever before, and fired. The projectiles shot through the air and blasted through the armor scales of the dragon's neck. Blood shot from the creature, but it didn't slow its descent. Bjorn fired again, and just like before, the arrows pierced the armored scales like they weren't even there. He kept this up until the dragon had enough and turned away. Bjorn checked the quiver. Less than five arrows were remaining. That strategy wouldn't work a second time. He spied the buried sword.

Bjorn dropped back to the opening and ran towards the sword. He was almost there when the dragon's shadow washed over him. He looked up and saw the beast's wide-open mouth aimed straight at him. The glow grew, and then there was a loud crack and a smash, and the monster fell. Bjorn looked back and saw Skadi standing, picking up a second bolder. She launched it into the air, and it came crashing down on the dragon.

She jumped and landed next to her son. The monster clawed at the ground and shook off the pain she had inflicted. It roared and flapped its mighty wings to once again take to the sky, but before it could get any distance, Skadi leaped and grappled the dragon by the upper neck and brought its head to the ground.

"You are a fearsome beast," she whispered. "It would be a shame for you to die today, Níðhöggr."

Bjorn looked at her curiously.

"It has a name?" he said.

The dragon tried to wrestle itself free. It flapped its wings, and Skadi tightened her hold.

"You've been bested, and we've already consumed the root. Live to fight another day," said Skadi.

Níðhöggr roared and blasted fire, but it quickly calmed and sighed. Cautiously, Skadi released her hold of the dragon then patted its neck. The creature turned to face Skadi and Bjorn. Bjorn took a defensive stance.

"It's all right," said Skadi.

She and the dragon locked eyes for a period, then it flapped its wings and shot into the air. The mother and son watched as the dragon disappeared behind the mountain then looked at one another.

"Did you know it?" said Bjorn.

"Of it," replied Skadi. "Let's keep moving. Where is my sword?"

MAKING PEACE

Hovard and Elfr rode in silence along the stretch of path that led alongside the Forest of Fate, the location of Urðarbrunnr. It was Elfr who broke the silence.

"We turn here," he said.

"Those men were not a threat," said Hovard.

"We gave them a reason to be. Vengeance is a powerful motivator. You should know this," said Elfr.

"Once I have done what I need to do, I will give this power back," said Hovard.

"Power can be a difficult thing to relinquish willingly," said Elfr.

The two men continued beside the forest and, for more time, rode in silence side by side. Hovard eyed the dwarven sword that Elfr hung from his waist. He knew Elfr was scanning his thoughts.

Nightfall came, and the sky was clear. The moon was out, as were the stars. It had been a long journey from Hlíðarendi, and they would need to rest soon. It would still be some time before they arrived at Urðarbrunnr.

"Let's set up camp here," said Hovard. "We will arrive tomorrow evening."

He stepped down from his horse and hitched it to a nearby tree. Elfr did the same and removed the contents of a bag for building a tent.

Hovard scouted a place on the ground not far from his horse, situated some kindling, and lit a fire using a small spark he produced by snapping his fingers.

"You have such mastery of your power already. That is impressive," said Elfr.

Hovard said nothing.

"It took me quite some time to know the extent of what I can do, but when I finally mastered my ability, I was elated," said Elfr.

Again, Hovard did not respond.

"Reading the minds of men and women proved helpful as a councilman, but it was the control over beasts that gave me real pleasure," said Elfr.

There was a rumbling that, despite Hovard's best attempt at ignoring Elfr, he could not ignore. The ground shook, and leaves fell from the trees. Hovard looked up and what he saw impressed him.

The urge to comment overwhelmed his desire to ignore Elfr, and he whispered, "Well, isn't that something."

The following morning, the two men packed up their things and continued their journey to Hvergelmir with hopes of cutting off Skadi and Bjorn. Little did they know that the mother and son would arrive with time to face Níðhöggr and acquire the root.

"Can I tell you something?" said Elfr.

"Why ask when you are going to say it anyway?" said Hovard.

"This is the most of Midgard I have ever seen. Believe it or not, but I have lived in Fensalir my entire life, and rarely have I gone more than a few miles outside of the town," Elfr admitted. "We all have never been too far outside of Fensalir. Each of the council members, I mean. All but Lofn. She is from Thrymheim."

"I am not surprised," said Hovard. "Many do not wish to venture outside of their towns. Midgard can be dangerous. People die every day in Midgard. Some for a good reason but many for not. But that is the risk you take. There is freedom here."

"When I first ran for town council, I thought I would root out the troubles of Fensalir, but I'm sure just as any leader might tell you, I instantly realized things were far more complicated than they had seemed, but despite that, we were making some headway. Me and the others who were elected," said Elfr.

"Are you talking just to talk?" said Hovard. "Or does this story have a point?"

"I'm sharing. I'm hoping you will, too," said Elfr.

"Can't you read my mind?"

"I can only go so deep, and you're especially difficult to read," Elfr said. "You don't trust me. I know. I don't trust you either, but we have a partnership, so I'm trying to make peace."

"Elfr, I will tell you this once and only once. I do not wish to be your friend. Once this mission is over, I do not wish ever to see you again. But I do not wish to be your enemy, so if you seek peace, then it is peace you will have. But do not dishonor me any further with your cowardice."

"I can shake on that," said Elfr.

Hovard extended his hand, and as the men rode on, their hands clasped one another's, and the agreement was bound.

"So, are you willing to tell me about yourself?" said Elfr.

"No," replied Hovard.

More time passed, and the sun began to set. The shadow of Hvergelmir was approaching, and in the distance, Hovard and Elfr could see a burst of red and yellow at the peak.

"What do you think that is all about?" said Elfr.

"Gnawing at the World Tree at Hvergelmir is the dragon Níðhöggr," said Hovard. "I believe Skadi, and Bjorn beat us here and are facing it as we speak."

"Maybe it'll do our job for us," said Elfr.

"Unlikely. Skadi is resilient, and she is doing this for her boy. That makes her equally as dangerous as the dragon."

"They're going to get the second root," said Elfr.

"Then we'll be waiting for them," said Hovard.

THE KNIFE CUTS DEEP

Liótr burst into the council chambers holding the swaddling blanket found at Frija's home. Dana was sitting at the large council table. He dropped the blanket down on the table in front of her. She looked at it, then up at him.

"What is this?" she said.

"You tell me. Do you know what is going on here?" He said.

"Relax. What have you found?" she asked.

"Frija is no witch," said Liótr. "She is—"

The door to the chamber opened. Dana looked beyond Liótr.

"Do not concern yourself with this. It makes no difference. Have your men gathered her belongings?" said the jötunn.

"We have," said Liótr. "Will her magic amplify your abilities?"

"Her magic is lost on me. Her runes will go to my son," said the jötunn.

"I didn't know you were a parent," said Dana.

"Because I did not tell you," said the jötunn.

"Is your son in Fensalir?" said Liótr.

"You need to find Frija and do not worry about her true nature. She has no power here," said the jötunn.

The creature exited, leaving Dana and Liótr alone around the conference table.

"I'm worried we are in over our heads," said Liótr.

"You heard him. We are in too deep to turn around now," said Dana.

Dana saw Liótr shift his gaze back towards the swaddling blanket. She grabbed it and tossed it to the floor.

"Find Frija. That's all you need to worry about," she said.

He nodded and exited the room.

Dana glanced at the blanket and whispered, "This is not good."

Liótr met up with his men outside of the town council building. The one knocked unconscious by Frija was nursing his injury, and the other two were standing by his side.

"No one is to speak of what they found at the witch's home," said Liótr. "Is that understood?"

"But sir, she isn't a witch. She is—"

"Not another word. No one is to speak of this," Liótr said.

There was slight grumbling, but the men didn't dare say anything further.

"She is a witch without access to her magic, so she is just as mortal as the rest of us. We'll find her and bring her to justice for the deaths of our town's children," said Liótr.

"Sir, I don't mean to be combative, but how are the four of us supposed to find her? Fensalir is not a big town, but it is not a small one either. There's plenty of places for her to hide and rebuild her stockpile of runes," said one of the men.

"I agree. Get the word out to the families of Fensalir, especially those who lost a child to this monster. Tell them she is hiding, and we need to establish search parties. We'll smoke her out," said Liótr. "And remember, not a word of what was found in her home. We don't need to cause a panic."

The three men nodded.

"Tell the families we will meet back here tomorrow morning and begin nonstop searches. No rock will be left unturned," said Liótr.

"Yes, sir," said the men in unison.

Frija ducked behind a nearby building, having heard the entire conversation between Liótr and his men.

"Search parties," she said. "Damn."

She peered around the corner, and Liótr and his men were gone. Frija snuck closer to the town council building, paying close attention to her surroundings so those searching would not find her. Upon arriving at the building, she placed small pieces of kindling wood at points crucial to the building's structural integrity. Placing the wood took only moments as she circled the entire complex.

"This should keep them preoccupied," she said and proceeded to light each of the kindling piles with a piece of flint and iron.

The fire quickly took hold of the council building and climbed the sides of the wooden structure, eventually engulfing the roof. Frija went back into hiding, having heard footsteps and voices approaching.

"Who did this?" shouted Liótr.

"It had to have been the witch," said one of his men.

"Dana, are you still inside?" shouted Liótr. "Dana, are you in there?"

He ran to the door, but it erupted in flames just as he got there. The fire forced him to step back.

"Dana," he shouted again.

"Sir, what are we going to do?" said one of his men.

"Get a bucket line going to the swamp. Do it now," said Liótr.

Dana stood inside of the council chamber, eager to make her escape but unwilling to alert anyone to her power.

"Stop yelling, you fool," she said as Liótr called her name from the other side of the council walls. "I'm here."

The fire was breaking through the exterior, and embers were burning inside the chamber.

Several volunteers arrived in town to form the bucket line, and soon there was a connection to Sökkvabekkr, but the water had yet to begin hitting the building. Dana moved from the chamber room to the hall.

Dana looked out of one of the building's few windows and saw the bucket line. She smashed her fist into her palm in frustration.

"Now I have to wait," she whispered.

Liótr circled the building looking for the window nearest Dana's last known location.

"Dana," he shouted.

"What is it, you fool?" she said, appearing in the window.

"Just making sure you're okay," he said.

"I'm fine. You should have given me time to get out of here before you called for the bucket line," she said.

"Sorry, I had to do something," he said.

"Leave the thinking to me. Frija did this to cause a distraction, and it's worked. We can't underestimate her cleverness, and there is no guarantee that Elfr and Hovard will be successful, which means we may soon be dealing with Skadi and her son. We must be cautious as we go forward. When you find Frija, I don't want you to subdue her; I want you to kill her. Do you understand?" said Dana.

"I do," said Liótr.

"I'm serious. Don't try and make an example out of her, don't prolong anything, don't monologue, just kill her. We can't afford to make any mistakes. This has become a delicate operation," she said.

"I get it," said Liótr.

"Then what are you doing still talking to me? Go," said Dana.

Liótr backed away from the building and grumbled, but he didn't dare speak against Dana so she could hear. He kept his remarks in his head at least until he was far enough away that he was sure she wouldn't hear.

"Everyone thinks I'm stupid. I'm not stupid. I know what I'm doing," he whispered.

"Sir, the bucket line is up and running. We'll have the fire put out in no time," said one of his men.

"Good. I'm going to follow up on Frija's whereabouts. You stay here and make sure this runs accordingly. The plan is still to have the families meet in the morning, so once the fire is extinguished, make sure you get the word out. Many of the people you'll need to talk to are part of the bucket line anyway," said Liótr.

"Yes, sir," said the man.

Liótr left the scene of the fire and retreated to his home. He fussed around in the drawer of his desk and pulled out the seeing-rune he'd secretly recovered from Frija's home.

"Not so dumb that I didn't think this would come in handy," he said.

He lifted the rune to his lips and closed his eyes.

"Find Frija," he whispered.

Immediately a bird's eye view of Fensalir appeared before him as if he were having the most vivid dream imaginable. The view scanned over the entire town, bouncing from place to place. Liótr's eyelids flickered like he was in REM sleep. This constant bouncing around continued for about three minutes before he realized he saw the same locations over again.

He opened his eyes and looked at the rune.

"This should be working," he said.

Frija sensed that someone was using one of her runes to find her and was glad she had the foresight to make herself immune to her own magic.

"I'm not far," said Frija. "The seeing-rune will come in handy to stay a step ahead of them once they organize search parties."

She threw on a cloak to cover her face and emerged onto a backroad of Fensalir. It would be only a few minutes until she arrived at Liótr's home.

Liótr fiddled with the rune, hitting it against his desk a few times.

He lifted it again to his lips and a second time uttered, "Find Frija."

Just as before, the bird's eye view of Fensalir bounced around the entire town, but it never landed on a single person.

"Piece of junk," he said and stuffed the rune in the desk drawer.

Liótr headed for the door, and as he stood in the doorway, he looked back at the desk.

Frija arrived at Liótr's home and saw him exiting. She stayed covered and was confident he didn't see her. When he was gone, she moved closer, remaining cognizant of her surroundings. Only feet away, she glanced all around her and made for the front door when the coast was clear. It was not locked.

She rummaged through his living room and bedroom before returning to the living room, where she saw his desk.

"That's it," she whispered and proceeded to pull open every drawer. There was nothing.

"Where is it?" she said.

"Looking for this?" said Liótr standing in the doorway.

Frija's heart sank upon hearing the councilman. She slowly turned around to face him.

"I had a sneaking suspicion it would alert you to my whereabouts, so I took it with me," he said, holding up the rune. "And people think I'm dumb for some reason."

"Liótr, don't do anything hasty," said Frija. "The jötunn is a terrible creature. What the council has done is despicable."

"Fully aware of that," said Liótr. "And it does not change a thing for me. You and your attack dog Skadi are all that stands in the way, and soon you won't be an issue."

As he stepped through the door into his home, Frija stepped backward.

"Easy, Liótr. There are forces at play bigger than you," said Frija.

"You don't scare me. I'm fully aware of who you are, and . . . I'm not phased. Dana and the jötunn have assured me that isn't a problem."

"And you trust them?" said Frija.

"More than you," said Liótr. "I trust Dana."

He stepped forward some more. Frija backed up in kind. Her palms were sweaty, and her heartbeat raced faster and faster.

"Fensalir deserves better than you all," said Frija. "I'm going to make sure of it."

"Good luck with that," said Liótr. "You're all alone here."

He lunged at her. His massive girth flew so fast she barely had time to react, but she managed to dodge him. His body slammed into the wall of his home and cracked it. Frija breathed in deeply. She could not afford even the slightest misstep.

He shook his head and looked back at her. Frija jumped for the front door, but Liótr launched into the air again. He cut off her escape.

"I can do this all day," he said. "You know what power the jötunn granted me?"

"I don't have time for this," said Frija.

"Strength," he answered. "And stamina."

Liótr closed the door behind him. Frija put up her hand and slowly backed away.

"Easy now," she said.

He charged at her as if he was a bull. Each of his steps pounded against the ground, shaking the foundation of the home. Frija had little time to react, but her quick thinking did her well. She threw a knife on the ground as Liótr stepped, and the blade went right through his foot. He screamed and fell to the ground. Frija made a wide orbit around him and ran out of the house.

Quickly she sought cover and spied on Liótr's home. She was watching to see if he would exit. Frija waited for about five minutes, but he never appeared. When she felt the coast was clear, she made her escape.

Liótr pulled the blade from his foot, wrapped it in bandages as best he could, and then nursed his wound.

"Don't try and make an example out of her, don't prolong anything, don't monologue, just kill her. We can't afford to make any mistakes," whispered Liótr, reiterating what Dana had said to him. "Fuck."

His foot was throbbing and served as a reminder that he had let her slip right through his fingers despite having her cornered in his home.

"I am not stupid," he told himself.

"But your actions speak otherwise," said Lofn.

Liótr turned around and saw his colleague standing in the doorway.

"What do you want?" he said.

"Dana doesn't think much of you. I'm sure you know that, but I overheard your conversation with her about the swaddling cloth, and I'm not sold on the idea that we shouldn't be concerned."

"What are you proposing?" said Liótr.

"That we cut our losses. What are we even doing this for anymore? Petronilla is dead, and for what?" said Lofn.

"We can't," said Liótr.

"I can summon and speak to the dead," said Lofn. "And believe me, you don't want to find yourself amongst them. Only the honorable go to Valhalla. We've done bad, but there may still be hope for us."

"The only hope for us is to resolve this situation we're in as quickly as possible. The jötunn will not be forgiving. Frija will not be forgiving. Skadi will not be forgiving. Our only option is to fight," said Liótr. "At least take ownership of the bad we've done. We have to see this through to the end."

"This will not end well for anyone," said Lofn. "Not you, not me, not the jötunn, not Skadi, not Frija, not anyone. The dead speak, and what they are telling me is that the end is coming."

"The end?"

"Fimbulwinter."

"Fimbulwinter is near?" said Liótr in disbelief.

Lofn nodded.

"You're sure?" Liótr said.

"Absolutely," said Lofn.

"Then if the Great Winter is nearly upon us, we better get our affairs in order," said Liótr. "What sort of creatures can you summon?"

"If they live in Hel and they are there because of me, then they are one of my draugr," said Lofn.

"Then get me something that can fly that's big enough for us to ride," said Liótr.

THE WORLD TROLL

"Let's rest here," said Skadi as they reached the halfway point down the mountain.

"But I'm not tired," said Bjorn.

"But I am," replied Skadi.

Skadi took a seat on a downed tree. She pulled out a flagon of water and took two large gulps. She looked at Bjorn, who was watching her, and extended the flagon towards him. He took it.

"What are we doing?" he said.

"What's it look like, son? We are resting," she said.

"But isn't time pressing?" he said.

"We are only a few hours away from the base, but something has me concerned," she said.

"What?" said Bjorn.

"It's just a feeling. I need to think. Take advantage of this opportunity to rest," she said.

"When did you hear of that dragon?" said Bjorn.

"My father told me about it when I was a child. He said it was a fearsome creature that gnawed at the roots of the World Tree," said Skadi.

"Grandpa," said Bjorn. "What was he like?"

"Son, let me think."

Skadi observed her son take a seat, fall on his back, and stare up at the sky. She noticed he was asleep almost immediately. While he was out, she started a fire and caught an animal to roast over it.

"How long was I out?" said Bjorn.

"Not long," she said.

She was lying. She had hours to think while he slept.

"It's late," he said.

"There is a trap waiting for us at the base of the mountain," said Skadi.

"How do you know?" said Bjorn.

"It's a feeling. The roots of the Yggdrasil have heightened all our senses. We aren't just stronger. We're more perceptive too. I caught this with my eyes closed," said Skadi pointing at the animal over the fire.

"And you think there is a trap waiting for us at the base of the mountain?"

"If not a trap, at least something dangerous. Every animal that has passed us has scurried uphill away from the base, and there is a very subtle temperature change. As we go down, it gets warmer despite the dragon being at the peak," said Skadi. "If you focus, you can sense it too."

"What could scare these animals more than a dragon?" said Bjorn.

"I don't know," said Skadi.

She pulled the animal off the fire and checked to make sure she cooked it thoroughly. Skadi tore a piece of meat and took a bite, then handed the rest to Bjorn.

"Eat up," she said. "I'm going to rest my eyes. When I awake, we'll spring the trap."

Night on the Hvergelmir Mountain was oddly peaceful. The stars were entirely visible despite a handful of clouds, and the moon was full. Bjorn tried to practice the heightened perception his mother told him they could perform. After a little while, he, too, could sense the movement of animals heading towards the peak. Even the smallest critters were detectable.

"It's as if I am experiencing Midgard for the first time," he whispered to himself.

Bjorn looked up at the night sky.

"Dad, are you watching?"

As the night faded to dawn, Skadi stirred then awakened. The fire had burned out, and she saw that Bjorn had fallen back asleep. Mildly annoyed, she shook him to wake up.

"Sorry," he said, immediately realizing what he'd done.

"It's fine," said Skadi. "It's better we are both at one hundred percent."

She stomped out the remains of the fire and took a sip of water from her flagon. Skadi passed it to Bjorn, and he did the same.

"Are you ready for whatever it is we'll face?" she said.

Bjorn nodded.

"I am," he said.

Just then, they both heard neighing and galloping. Bjorn's horse that Hrimthur had given him came darting towards them. It was dragging the piece of tree it had been tied to when they first arrived.

"Well, look at that," said Skadi.

She mounted the horse ahead of Bjorn and assisted him to the back. She waited for him to wrap his arms around her waist, and she squeezed the sides of the horse to get the creature moving. Not before long, they were charging down the side of the mountain.

Hovard and Elfr waited patiently on opposite sides of an open plain at the base of Hvergelmir behind a large boulder and a massive tree. In Elfr's hand was Dáinsleif. In Hovard's hand, there was nothing, and that was the most dangerous possession of all.

Elfr's was nervous, and his heart was racing. However, he was ready. Hovard, on the other hand, was calm. He focused his mind as he prepared to lead the charge.

The two made eye contact when they heard the galloping hooves of Skadi and Bjorn approaching. They nodded at each other and waited.

Skadi and her son raced off the mountain towards the opening where Hovard and Elfr prepared for their ambush, then she pulled hard on the reins, and the horse nearly skidded to a stop as an explosion kicked up dirt and debris ahead of them. Quickly, Skadi grabbed Bjorn and leaped from the horse as a fireball flew overhead. It crashed behind them, erupting in a fiery blast of energy and dirt that washed over the mother and son.

She quickly scrambled to their feet, pulled Bjorn up, and retreated into the woods at the start of the mountain incline.

"Is the dragon back?" said Bjorn.

"That wasn't the dragon. That was something else."

"Skadi," shouted Hovard. "Come out now."

A wave of fire tore into the tree line, eating up the forest. It quickly eradicated the covering that Skadi and Bjorn were using to hide. Skadi pulled Bjorn back some more to evade the fire torching them to death.

"Call your horse," said Skadi.

Bjorn whistled, but the response he received was anything but what he desired. The horse came to him, but it didn't gallop. It flew through the air after being thrown by a gargantuan mountain troll. It tumbled to a stop at Bjorn's feet, pulverized into a bloody mess.

"I said come out," shouted Hovard.

She looked at Bjorn. He shook his head. But she stepped from behind the tree that covered her. She had her hands raised over her head.

"Hovard," she said.

"Skadi."

Hovard stood in the shadow of the mountain troll. The giant beast hunched over him, both protecting him and ready to attack. Hovard's hands were glowing.

"What are you doing here?" said Skadi.

"You didn't think you would see me again?" he said.

"To be honest, no," she said.

"I always knew I would see you again," said Hovard.

"Well, here I am," Skadi said.

Skadi checked Hovard's hands that glowed with a raging fire. As if in anticipation of the attack, she dodged left, avoiding that wave of fire that came shooting towards her. The fire cut down trees and superheated the air around her. She evaded by ducking, dodging, jumping, and hiding, and after a while, he stopped.

"Where did you get this power?" Skadi shouted.

"It was a gift," he said.

Skadi spied Bjorn turn his attention to Hovard and the mountain troll.

"Don't engage," she shouted, but her words fell on deaf ears as he picked up a large rock on the ground and chucked it at Hovard.

The rock moved through the air lightning-fast, but the troll put a hand down in front of Hovard and blocked it. The rock disintegrated upon impact, but the troll hardly flinched. The beast looked in Bjorn's direction, as did Hovard, as did Skadi.

The troll was much larger than the one they had faced only a few days prior, and that one had given them a lot of trouble. It nearly crippled Bjorn. But since that bout, they had consumed two of the three Yggdrasil roots. Maybe they stood a fighting chance. But then again, the heat emanating from Hovard was hotter and fiercer than that of the dragon Níðhöggr.

"Take him," said Hovard.

The troll started moving in Bjorn's direction, and every step shook the ground. Hovard refocused on Skadi. Skadi prepared for another overwhelming wave of fire that blasted through her covering. She ducked, rolled, and bounced to her feet to avoid the blast. Hovard again let up his attack, and Skadi was still standing. The trees that surrounded the open plain, however, were all decimated and smoldering. The once lush plant life that grew at the mountain base now resembled the inside of a forge with embers burning all around. Skadi was sweating, and her pelts were scorched, but she was okay. She drew her sword and prepared to counter.

While Skadi was preoccupied with Hovard, Bjorn was trying his hardest to defeat the powerful troll. He drew an arrow from his quiver and pulled back as hard as he could, and the unbelievable happened—the bow snapped. He looked at the weapon in disbelief and chucked the remains to the ground.

The troll picked up its pace, closing the gap between it and Bjorn. Bjorn looked behind him, and his back was against a steep cliff face. Bjorn breathed in deep and sighed a heavy sigh, then clenched his hands into fists.

The loud boom caught the attention of everyone on the battlefield. The troll was stumbling backward as Bjorn descended to the ground with his right fist still raised in the air. He was holding his wrists but what had happened was obvious. He had just knocked the creature to the ground with one punch. The weight of the troll shook the earth beneath everyone's feet.

"That's impossible," whispered Elfr, having witnessed the whole thing from his hiding spot.

Bjorn landed and immediately charged the creature as it was attempting to regain its footing. He leaped and tackled the troll and began savagely pounding on its face. Every hit bloodied the beast more and more until the troll stopped struggling, and blood covered Bjorn like he was like a feral animal that had just captured and killed its prey.

He was breathing rapidly, almost hyperventilating, but he climbed off the troll and stood between it and Hovard.

"That was . . . impressive," said Hovard as he raised a hand in Bjorn's direction.

"No," shouted Skadi, before throwing her sword.

Bjorn watched Hovard react quickly and attempt to melt the sword before it reached him, but a shard made it just far enough and cut his hand. He yelled and grabbed his hand. Blood streamed through his right hand, but he used his powers to cauterize the wound.

"Enough," whispered Elfr.

The ground shook, stronger than before. It rumbled and quaked violently, growing in severity by the second. Then over the ridge appeared the silhouettes of four massive mountain trolls, each bigger than the one before.

"If it's a fight you want. It's a fight you'll get," said Elfr, finally stepping from his hiding place.

The mountain trolls lined up alongside one another, casting a long, wide shadow on the battlefield. It was a shadow that was suddenly whisked away by the glow coming from Hovard. Flame engulfed him, and his eyes were burning red.

Skadi started running towards Hovard; he unleashed his flames. Skadi leaped into the air with such force, the ground where she launched from cratered. Hovard followed her trajectory into the blinding sun. He lost her in the light, and when she reappeared, she was in his face, fist ready for impact. Hovard dropped to a knee, grabbed her arm, and used her momentum against her, tossing her body over his into the dirt. She bounced off the ground but quickly retaliated. He propelled himself backward using the fire that came from him like jets.

Skadi looked right and saw an enormous boulder. She dug her fingers into the rock and pulled it free from the ground. With what strength she could muster, she launched it in the air after Hovard. He blasted it, and it exploded into a thousand little pieces, but through the explosion came Skadi. Hovard's eyes went wide. She had him. Then she stopped and was slammed into the ground. One of the trolls had her by the ankle.

Hovard caught his breath. He thought that was it. Skadi kicked at the troll's hand, and it released her. But another picked her up and slammed her into the ground. The troll repeatedly bashed Skadi into the dirt, over and over until she managed to get a handle on the troll's colossal hand and twisted it until it broke. The troll screamed in pain and grabbed its hand. Skadi escaped from under the troll, leaped into its gut, and took the creature to the ground. She stomped the troll's face until its eyes bulged from its sockets, and she knew it was dead.

The trolls were Bjorn's priority. The first to reach him swiped at the boy, but he punched the creature's hand, snapping a finger. The beast yelled, but it didn't slow down. He swept its other hand through the dirt to grab the child, but Bjorn jumped over the other hand and kicked the creature in the ankle, taking it to the dirt. He moved to finish the troll like he finished the first with multiple punches to the face, but a second troll drew back its foot to kick Bjorn. Bjorn blocked, but the force was enough to send him flying. He landed on the ground many feet away, tumbled to a stop, and wiped sweat and blood from his face. He grinded his teeth and charged back in.

Bjorn crisscrossed three trolls, weaving in and out of their legs, forcing them to contend with each other's size and girth. He then punched the back of one's knee, causing the troll to lose its balance and fall into the other two. On its way down, Bjorn ran up the monster's back, grabbed it by the back of its head, and smashed his own head into the troll's. Blood burst from its skull. Bjorn hit it again and again and again until the troll's skull cracked. The creature hit the ground, and Bjorn jumped off it.

"You're going to have to do better than that," shouted Bjorn.

"I think I can," said Elfr.

The ground quaked greater than before with a constant reverberation that caught the attention of Skadi, Bjorn, Hovard, and even the two remaining trolls. They all looked to see what was approaching.

A hand appeared at the edge of the battlefield, followed by an enormous face, then a neck and a body. Legs followed. Something massive was rising from over the ledge. It towered over the two surviving trolls on the battlefield, four times their height and width.

Bjorn looked up at the monster that towered overhead. He'd never seen a creature this big. He had never even known creatures like this existed. At least not in Midgard—maybe in Jotunheim, where the giants lived.

"What is that?" said Bjorn.

"A world troll," said Elfr. "A creation of the mad god who long ago coerced a group of giants to lay with trolls."

The two normal-sized trolls, by comparison, once again turned their attention on Bjorn. Hovard, too, returned his focus to Skadi.

"Despite your power boosts, this is not a winnable fight. You haven't changed at all. You still think there is a way despite the odds," said Hovard.

"There is always a way, Hovard," said Skadi. "That's what you never understood."

"You turned your back on your family."

"You didn't want to let us go," shouted Skadi.

"And now you'll pay dearly," said Hovard.

The two mountain trolls and the world troll started in on Bjorn. He battled the smaller ones, dispatching them at no greater difficulty than the others, but the world troll sent shockwaves through Midgard with every step, and when it punched, Bjorn went flying. Not only was the creature strong, but it was also fast. He crashed to the ground many feet away.

"Get up," said Skadi, turning towards him

"Mom, my leg," said Bjorn.

Crashing into the ground had snapped Bjorn's leg just below the knee. He could no longer fight.

"It's over," said Hovard.

The whinny of Bjorn's horse surprised Skadi as the creature galloped over and stood between her, Bjorn, and Hovard. She grabbed Bjorn and tossed him over the saddle and leaped up herself.

"Yah," she shouted, and the horse took off.

A wave of fire chased after them but just barely missed as they turned the corner of the mountain, out of sight of everyone. Skadi looked back just in time to see him launch into the air to surveil from up high, but he could not find them.

"That could have gone better," said Elfr after Hovard landed.

"The boy's leg is broken. They won't get far," Hovard said.

Skadi and Bjorn took refuge within a nearby cave.

"Bite this," she said to Bjorn and handed him her belt.

He bit down, and she carefully but quickly snapped his leg back in place. Skadi caught his head as he fell back, passed out from the pain.

Skadi was sitting with her back against the wall when he awoke, his leg bandaged.

"He did say the horse would heal from almost anything," said Bjorn.

"If only Eir had blessed you the same way," said Skadi.

"Who was that man?" said Bjorn. "How did he know you?"

"His name is Hovard Hervor," said Skadi. "He is my uncle."

"He's family?" said Bjorn.

"Hardly."

"Why is he after you?" said Bjorn.

"When your father and I decided to leave, Hovard believed we were turning our back on him and the clan we rode with. He operates by his own code, and now he seeks retribution. He must have tracked us to Fensalir," said Skadi.

"And was gifted powers by the jötunn," said Bjorn.

NINETEEN

BUNA AND ALVER

Buna sat with her husband in her new council quarters, having just taken the oath of office and made her first vote as a councilwoman for Fensalir. Liótr and the others scurried off upon having made the vote, leaving the wife and husband alone. A pot of tea was brewing on the stove in the corner.

"Do you think I made the right decision?" said Buna.

"Yes," said Alver.

"It feels rushed and drastic," she said.

"We're in a crisis," said Alver. "That's just how things are in a crisis."

The tea kettle started to whistle. She got up from her seat, walked over, and took it off the heat.

As she fiddled with the loose-leaf tea, she said, "Frija has lived here longer than the kids started being killed. I remember seeing her around when we first arrived. That was long before Dofri."

"And what's your point?" said Alver.

"Why hadn't the killings been happening before if it was Frija? Why wasn't it an ongoing problem before we arrived if she was already here?" said Buna.

"Maybe she didn't start until later," said Alver.

"Maybe. But . . . that doesn't strike you as odd?" said Buna.

"No," said Alver. "When I was still a boy, I once saw a man I had known for years who had been a peaceful man as far as I knew, kill his wife and then himself. No one knew why he did it or what changed, but just that one day he had been one way and the next he had been another way. I think that people can just change like that."

"I believe you," said Buna. "But it still seems odd that she would have lived here for so long without there being any incidents then suddenly start killing kids in a patterned way," said Buna. "That is odd."

Alver shrugged.

"I don't know," he said. "Maybe something suspicious is happening then."

"I'm going to look into it. If I voted wrong, that is on me, but I can at least try and make things right," she said.

"I love your commitment to justice, but maybe you're getting ahead of yourself. Let them capture Frija, and if she is found not guilty, then I will help you with finding the real killer, but if she is found guilty, then . . ." said Alver.

"Then what? Fensalir has a history of mob justice," said Buna. "I just participated in it. I let them talk me into something without really being shown any proof. How do we know that if they capture her, she'll get a fair trial? Remember what happened to Jon, who got accused of stealing? Sometimes we react before we think, and the wrong people get really hurt."

"I don't know," said Alver.

"None of this is sitting right with me," said Buna.

"So, how do we go about this?" Alver said. "What happens next?"

"First thing is we don't trust these council members anymore. Not until we've properly vetted them," said Buna. "And the second thing is we go look at Frija's home for clues as to who she really is."

"Okay," said Alver.

"And the third thing we do is . . ." said Buna.

"What?" said Alver.

"Oh, my Odin," said Buna.

"What is it?" said Alver.

She slowly raised her hand and pointed behind him. The door had opened and standing in the doorway was the jötunn.

"What is that?" she said.

Alver turned around and quickly jumped to his feet between the jötunn and Buna.

"You have served your purpose, but we can't have you snooping around," said the creature.

"Buna, get out of here," shouted Alver.

The jötunn swiftly pushed Alver aside. He fell into the chairs on which they had been sitting. The monster then moved in on Buna. She stumbled backward, scrambling to get away from the massive creature.

"Get away from me," she shouted.

"Buna, run," shouted Alver.

She looked behind her, but there was nowhere to go. She was trapped. Walls were around her, and the door was behind the monster. Buna's heart raced but then quickly slowed as the jotunn stabbed her through the abdomen with his claws.

"Your deductive reasoning was impressive," said the jötunn.

"What . . . are you?" she said, coughing up blood.

"I am just someone trying to survive like the rest of you," said the jötunn.

A cracking sound ripped through the room as a beam came crashing down in the hallway, and a wave of heat flooded over everyone. The fire that Frija started was spreading.

The jötunn withdrew its hand from Buna's body. Life was draining from her fast. She looked at her husband. He was attempting to get up. She slowly shook her head.

"Don't think I've forgotten about you," said the jötunn without looking his way.

Buna stumbled backward and fell to one knee.

"I've made a mistake," she whispered.

The jötunn leaned over, so its face was directly in front of hers.

"That you have," he said.

The jötunn stood up and pushed aside the fallen beam that blocked the room's exit. The fire raged all around him. His eyes were red, and his right hand was stained with Buna's blood. Her body lay behind him, starting to catch fire. The room was engulfed, and smoke was clouding it. Another beam crashed, and the heat intensified tenfold. The jötunn looked back at Alver, and to his surprise, he was gone. Fire flooded the room.

"These humans are becoming problematic," the creature whispered before exiting.

Alver did not stop running until the smoke cloud ascending from the town council building was so far away that it looked like an incense candle burning. He leaned against a tree and rested his hands on his knees. Alver fought the urge to yell but could not control the tears that streamed down his face.

"Buna," he said. "What was that?"

He wiped his tears and stood up straight.

"I have to find Frija," he said. "I have to for Buna, for Dofri."

Liótr took a step back from Lofn as she made a series of hand gestures, and the ground around them started to shake. The dirt directly before them separated, and from it emerged a half-decomposed bird. It was a massive creature with a wingspan nearly thirty feet long.

"I think this should be sufficient," said Lofn with a subtle smile.

"You're coming with me. We're going to track this witch down and be done with this—together," said Liótr.

He mounted the bird and extended his hand.

"I said this does not end well," said Lofn.

"We're all walking towards the same destination," said Liótr. "The only question is how do we get there? We chose this path."

Lofn nodded and took his hand. "Fine. But for the record, you will see that I am right."

"I'm sure."

The undead bird flapped its massive wings and carried the two council members into the sky. They ascended so high they could see all Fensalir. They had an angle at that moment that they only shared with the god at the peak of Himinbjorg.

"Keep an eye out," said Liótr. "She's around here somewhere."

Alver walked briskly through the forest on the outskirts of Fensalir, not quite sure where he was heading but with the thought that he should not stop moving. He looked up when he heard the loud caw of what had to be a giant bird and saw off in the distance, Liótr and Lofn taking to the sky.

"That's fucking strange," he whispered and took cover behind a tree.

He watched them fly overhead and made sure to hug the tree, so the branches obfuscated their view of him. They flew off, and the silhouette of the bird grew smaller and smaller.

"What is going on in this town?"

TWENTY

ODIN'S ADVISOR

Bjorn sat with his back against the wall of the cave. Both he and Skadi felt the tremors of the world troll's steps, but with each succeeding tremor, its strength faded, meaning the troll was moving away from their location, and with it, Hovard and Elfr.

"Just a little bit longer," said Skadi.

"Mom, are we going to be able to do this?" asked Bjorn. "Your uncle and that other guy . . . they were strong."

"We're strong too."

"But we've consumed two of the Yggdrasil roots and still were no match for them."

"We were a match," said Skadi. "We were just ambushed."

"And now I'm hurt, so if we go out there and they're still here, then we're going to lose," said Bjorn.

"We're not going out just yet, Bjorn. We can rest for a moment."

"But mom—"

"No buts," said Skadi. "They're moving away. We have time."

"But mom—"

"What did I say?"

"I know, but don't you think they're moving away so they can beat us to the final root?" said Bjorn. "Otherwise, wouldn't they stick around to look for us?"

"That . . . is a good point."

Bjorn tried shifting his weight so he could stand up.

"What are we going to do?" he said.

"Listen son," said Skadi standing up. "This last leg of this journey I need to do myself. I'm putting my foot down. For you, this journey is over," said Skadi.

"But mom—"

"No buts.

"I told the Norns I'm fighting for everyone, and I am, but everyone still includes you, and if something were to happen to you . . ."

"Mom," said Bjorn starting to protest. "I get it."

"I want you to take the horse back to Hlíðarendi and stay with Eir. After I get the final root, I will come to get you, and we'll both return to Fensalir together. By then, we'll be strong enough to take on the jötunn and all the council members," said Skadi.

Bjorn saw his mom extend her hand, and he took it so he could get to his feet. Together they hobbled to the horse. At this point, the tremors of the world troll were hardly noticeable.

"Ride safe, son, and tell Eir thank you," she said.

Bjorn nodded.

"Mom," he said. "I love you."

Skadi put a hand on his shoulder.

"I love you too. Now go," she said.

"Yah," said Bjorn, and the horse took off.

Bjorn looked back at his mother until she was no longer in sight, finally turning his attention forward. He rode through the day and then the night, his leg throbbing and the desire to rest tugging at the edges of his mind. His horse didn't tire as he did, and he couldn't afford to fall asleep for fear of falling off. He persisted and eventually saw Hlíðarendi on the horizon.

At that same time Bjorn was heading to Hlíðarendi, Skadi made for Mímisbrunnr, paying close attention to where she thought Hovard, Elfr, and the world troll were moving. Step after step brought her closer to the final root of the World Tree, but it also brought her closer to an inevitable confrontation that she was not sure she would win. Hovard and Elfr had proven themselves, and she had not.

The forest through which she traveled was dense, and without a horse, her movements were slow. She could speed things up, but she would exhaust herself, and she did not want to get caught by Hovard and Elfr or anything else this deep into uncharted Midgard, at anything other than her peak. Power boost or not, these lands were teeming with creatures that liked to feed on humans.

The sounds of the night were all around her, and with her heightened senses, she tried to read them to tell if danger lurked. Of course, it did, but to her surprise, it kept its distance. It occurred to Skadi that she was the alpha.

She moved uninhibitedly for quite some time until something caught her attention. It was a voice she heard that stopped her in her tracks. It was not just a voice; someone called her name from the shadows.

"Skadi," said the voice.

She stopped and looked around.

"Who said that?"

"Skadi Hervor," the voice repeated.

She scanned in all directions. There was no one to be seen.

"Down here," said the voice. "By the big tree ahead of you."

Skadi looked around her. She looked and saw the top of a man's head. It was just her and this man.

"Who are you?" said Skadi.

"Help me," said the man. "I cannot move."

"No one comes to this part of Midgard, not even Vikings or raiders. How did you get here?" she said.

"I have been in these lands for centuries. Since the Aesir-Vanir War. The name is Mimir," said the man.

"Mimir?" said Skadi.

"Please help me," said Mimir.

Skadi walked over, and to her surprise, she did not see a body attached to the head. She knelt and turned Mimir around to face her.

"What are you? How are you still alive?" said Skadi.

"I'm afraid your friends have beaten you to Mímisbrunnr," said Mimir. "I was there when they arrived. The one named Elfr commanded his troll to throw me away. That is how I landed here."

"But how are you alive without a body?" said Skadi.

"Seidr magic," said Mimir. "I'm of the Aesir."

"You're an Aesir God?" said Skadi, subtle surprise and shock entering her voice.

"A god might be a bit much, but I definitely once lived amongst the Aesir in Asgard. I was an advisor to Odin during the War, but when I was no longer of use, they exchanged me for Kvasir to live amongst the Vanir. However, the Vanir turned on me, and that was when I was beheaded."

Skadi picked up Mimir's and stood up.

"An advisor to Odin?"

She turned him over, scanning his neck. There was no opening, just skin.

"One might consider this inspection a bit rude," said Mimir.

She righted him.

"Even the Aesir need their bodies. This must be quite the magic."

"It is. I am a centuries-old head, after all."

Skadi smiled. It was her first smile in a very long time.

"The Aesir can be deviant gods . . . if you advised them, it is probably best I put you out of your bodiless misery."

"Wait," said Mimir. "You don't want to do that."

"Why wouldn't I?"

"Because I can help you. Elfr and Hovard are powerful . . . too powerful for you at the moment, but I can advise you on how to defeat them."

"Tell me why I should listen to you. I don't know you."

"Because if you don't, then Frija's plan to save Fensalir ends as soon as you get to Mímisbrunnr."

"You know Frija?"

"I do, and I know about her plan. She contacted me with a rune to seek my advice before she approached you."

Skadi stared at Mimir for what seemed an eternity.

"Frija came to you seeking advice on approaching me?"

"She did. She wanted to be sure you were up to this task. Frija cares about those people in Fensalir, and she wants you to be successful."

"If you're not an Aesir, then what are you?"

"Not all things fall neatly into defined categories, Skadi. Like a jötunn, I fall outside of any well-defined species. But if it makes you feel better, you can think of me as a demi-god."

"In time, hopefully, I can think of you as a friend. If Frija trusted you, then perhaps you can be an advisor to me. How do I defeat Elfr and Hovard and get the final root of the Yggdrasil?" she said.

Mimir laughed.

"I know we just went through all that back forth, and as much as I would like to get the bastards who tossed me aside, I can't just offer my services to you free of charge. Even Odin had to pay a price," said Mimir.

"You told me you would help to spare your life."

"That was to keep you from making a rash decision. But I'm not a charity."

"I take back what I said about becoming a friend. What do you want?" said Skadi.

"If I help you, I need you to swear a blood oath you will help me recover my original body," said Mimir.

"And what sage advice will I receive in return?" said Skadi.

"I will show you where to get a weapon that will defeat Dáinsleif, and I will reveal the location of the Yggdrasil Root at Mímisbrunnr using Odin's eye. That second one you were always going to need," said Mimir."

"What is so dangerous about Dáinsleif?" said Skadi.

"It is always lethal. No matter the size of the wound, being cut by Dáinsleif will mean certain death. The wound will not heal," said Mimir.

"And this is the weapon that they have?" said Skadi.

"Forged by your friend Bo using dwarven metal," said Mimir. "He meant for it to help Eir defeat Hovard."

"If he meant for it to help Eir, and yet it is now in the hands of Elfr and Hovard, then does that mean . . ." said Skadi.

"Yes. It means that they won and that Eir is dead. These two killed a Valkyrie," said Mimir.

"Bjorn."

"Your son will be fine. He should arrive there soon and realize that Eir is not there, but Hlíðarendi is safe for now," said Mimir.

"For now?"

"The Great Winter is approaching. Perhaps on your journey, you have noticed the creatures of Midgard acting strangely?" said Mimir. "Those are the early indicators of Fimbulwinter."

"How long do we have?" said Skadi.

"That I do not know. It could be days, weeks, months, or years but I do know it is coming and soon, relative to the lifespan of mortals, which means it is knocking on the door for the Gods," said Mimir.

"All right then, head. We do not have time to waste."

She used a knife to make a small cut on the palm of her hand.

"Where do you want it?" she said.

"Smear it across my forehead," said Mimir.

Skadi did as instructed then wiped the remaining blood on her pelt.

"We have a deal. I will show you how and where to get a weapon to defeat Dáinsleif as well as show you the final root of Yggdrasil, and in exchange, you will help me regain my original body," said Mimir.

"What do we have to do first?" said Skadi.

"Not what do we have to do but rather where do we have to go," said Mimir. "We must visit a dwarf named Reginn. He is the only dwarf who lives in Midgard. He has a sword called Ridill that will be powerful enough to defend against Dáinsleif and maybe even strike down the jötunn."

"How far away does this dwarf live?"

"Not far. If you run with your heightened abilities, you will be there in a day's time."

"Mimir, I'm going out of my way here. If this turns out to be a fool's errand, I will make—"

"I know. Trust me. What I'm telling you is the truth. I want my body back. You can't imagine the agony of being the wisest man alive and being confined to a single location for centuries. Odin cursed me to this fate the same way he has cursed others."

"I trust you," said Skadi. "But don't make me regret it."

TWENTY-ONE

WE ARE NOT JUST KIDS

"Mom should be arriving in Mímisbrunnr by now," said Bjorn as he limped alongside his horse.

He had just arrived in Hlíðarendi, and the first thing he noticed was the battlefield where Eir and Hovard faced.

"What happened here?"

Bjorn inspected the scorched ground. He knelt and ran the soil through his fingers.

"Was Hovard here?" he whispered.

"Hey, you," a man shouted from the gates of Hlíðarendi.

Bjorn stood up and turned around. A guard was standing at the top of the gate, staring down at him.

"Who are you? What are you doing here?" the guard said.

"My name is Bjorn Hervor. I was sent here to speak with Eir," he said.

"There is no Eir here," said the guard. "Not anymore, at least. You best keep going. We are not open to passersby."

"What happened?" said Bjorn.

"We still don't know," said the guard. "You better keep on. We're not taking in any outsiders."

"What about Bo and Hrimthur? I need to talk to them as well. Where are they?" asked Bjorn.

"Same story, friend. Both gone," said the guard.

"Both gone?" whispered Bjorn. "Killed?"

"You should leave, child," the guard said.

"Are they dead? That can't be," whispered Bjorn. "We were just here. If Hovard and that man killed a Valkyrie, is mom going to be able to do this on her own?"

"Kid are you hurt?" shouted the guard.

"My leg is broken," said Bjorn.

The guard grumbled. Bjorn could see the internal struggle he was facing.

"We have a healer who trained under Eir. She'll fix you right up. But then you must go," said the man.

"I will," said Bjorn.

A moment later, the gate opened and out stepped a young woman. She cautiously approached Bjorn, and he raised his hands to convey he was harmless.

"My name is Eirdóttir," said the young woman. "I will heal you, but once I do, please leave."

"You have my word," said Bjorn.

Eirdóttir reached Bjorn, and his horse neighed and lowered its head to be patted, something Bjorn noticed it never did for him. She rubbed its head and rustled its hair.

"May I ask you a question?" said Bjorn as the girl got near.

"Yes, you may," she said.

"Eir . . . was she your mother?" said Bjorn.

The girl nodded.

"She was," said Eirdóttir.

"I'm sorry," said Bjorn.

"You didn't do this," she said. "Please lie down."

Eirdóttir grabbed Bjorn's hand and assisted him to the ground. He lied down on his back with his legs outstretched. He remained still while she undid the bandages that Skadi had placed on him.

"My mother wanted to help you. She made her choice and determined her own fate," said Eirdóttir. "I am not as brave as her, but I want to help you too."

Bjorn felt the warmth of her hands as they hovered over his broken leg. Immediately the bone began to mend, and a sense of relief washed over him. It did not take long for him to heal fully, and he was up again within moments.

"Thank you," said Bjorn. "Your mother gave up being a Valkyrie for you. Is that true?"

"She did. When I was born, she chose to live as a woman . . . a healer. But it meant being ostracized. Her fellow Valkyries thought she had turned her back on them, but she had only chosen to give me a peaceful life. But in the end . . ."

"In the end, she gave her life to foster peace," said Bjorn.

"Your mother was a Viking warrior," said Eirdóttir. "It must not have been easy going her own way to raise you."

"I . . . suppose not," said Bjorn.

"What our parents do for us is never appreciated until it is too late," said Eirdóttir looking off in the distance.

Bjorn grabbed the reins of his horse and stepped one foot into the stirrup.

"Thank you for your help," he said. "What you and your mom did will never be forgotten."

"I'm coming with you," she said.

"What?" said Bjorn.

"I'm coming with you," she repeated. "To Fensalir. I know that is where you're heading. You're wondering if your mom will be enough to stop the men who attacked here, and if she isn't, then Fensalir will still be subject to the horrible jötunn, and it'll be up to you. I know that's what you are thinking, so I'll help. My mom told me what Frija told her about Fensalir."

"I don't think you should. This creature is powerful and has an entire town held hostage. I can't ask you to put yourself in harms' way like that," said Bjorn.

"Good because you're not asking me. I'm telling you that I will help," said Eirdóttir.

"It's going to be dangerous," said Bjorn.

"I'm aware. Fensalir gets ignored because its population is largely impoverished, and few care about the town, hence why it was the perfect place for a jötunn to take advantage of the people. My mom once said good people must do something or bad people will take everything. Besides, my father was from Fensalir, so it's just as much my home as it is yours," said Eirdóttir.

"I can't argue with your reasoning," Bjorn said.

He hopped up into the saddle and pulled Eirdóttir up after him.

"Hey," shouted the guard at the gate. "Where are you going?"

"With him," shouted Eirdóttir. "It's what my mother would have wanted."

"What your mother would have wanted is for you to stay here where it is safe," shouted the man.

"We can't stay hidden from danger forever," shouted Eirdóttir. "Eventually, we will all have to face it, but it is up to us to figure out how."

"You ready?" said Bjorn.

"Let's go," said Eirdóttir.

TWENTY-TWO

THE OLD DWARF

Frija took refuge in a cave near the edge of town. In the hours since her forced removal from her home, she had been on the constant run, never allowed to break for more than a few minutes. She had not felt this exhausted and pushed to her limits in a very long time.

"This is insane," she said, standing at the edge of the cave, looking up at the skies.

The undead bird cawed, and Frija ducked inside. She saw it fly over and observed Lofn and Liótr scanning the area.

"These two are a problem," she whispered.

Frija sat down with her back to the wall of the cave, ran her fingers through her hair, and let out a deep sigh.

"Come on, Skadi. I'm counting on you. Fensalir is counting on you," she said.

Holding Mimir's head, Skadi kept a pace that even the fastest horses would have envied. She ran over foliage, weaved around trees, and evaded creatures that would have loved to snack on a human far too deep into the darkest territories of Midgard.

"Tell me, Mimir, as an advisor to Odin, what would you advise him on?" said Skadi as she ran.

"All sorts of things," said Mimir. "He wasn't one for fashion, always opting for an old cloak and a hat and a tired old beard that made him look like a vagabond. I wanted him to update his style, but—"

"Seriously," said Skadi.

"War," said Mimir. "I advised Odin on ways to beat the Vanir. Sometimes he heeded my advice, and other times he did not. As you know, Midgard is but one of nine realms, and the Vanir and the Aesir both sought to control all of them."

"And the Aesir won that war, did they not?" said Skadi.

"Odin led a giant army to attack Vanaheim, but the Vanir were well prepared for his attack, and the battle ended in a stalemate. Both sides incurred massive damage and many casualties, which was only the first of hundreds of battles. The Vanir would learn that the Asgardians were just as capable of defending their lands, and over time both sides realized this was not a war to be won," said Mimir.

"So, they called a truce?"

"Of sorts," said Mimir. "They exchanged hostages to ensure peace. That is why today, some Vanir now live in Asgard, and some Asgardians live in Vanaheim."

"I didn't know that."

"Compromise, my mortal friend. Even the gods are forced to do it from time to time," said Mimir.

"What gods went where?" said Skadi.

"Well, let's see, the Vanaheim sent Njörðr and his son Freyr, and the Asgardians sent Hœnir and of course yours truly."

"What about Kvasir? You said earlier that you were exchanged for this god," said Skadi.

"Kvasir, like me, was not really a god, but he did live amongst them," said Mimir. "His origin is quite strange even by the standards of the nine realms. You see, when the Aesir and the Vanir called it a truce, they marked their truce by mixing their saliva in a vat. Afterward, Odin thought it a waste to leave the spittle and suggested they make something. Kvasir was what they made. He was the wisest man in the land at the time, even surpassing me, but I'm still here, and he is not."

"What happened to him?" said Skadi.

"A story for another time," said Mimir. "We are here."

Skadi slowed then stopped as they approached a humble cottage, set alone in a vast valley. Smoke billowed from its chimney into the black sky. She walked up to the cottage's front door with Mimir in hand and knocked twice.

"Who is it?" a voice said from within the home.

"Reginn, it's me, Mimir. Open up."

There was the sound of rummaging as the dwarf stumbled through his home. Moments later, the door opened, revealing a short, stocky fellow with a long grey beard and weathered eyes.

"You're not . . ." said Reginn.

Skadi held up Mimir's head before Reginn could complete his statement.

"Mimir," said Reginn. "Where is your body?"

"Long story," said Mimir. "May we come in?"

"Who's your friend?" said Reginn.

"Skadi Hervor," said Skadi.

"She needs your help with something," said Mimir.

Reginn looked Skadi up and down.

"She looks mean," he said.

"She isn't," said Mimir.

Reginn hesitated, then stepped aside, gesturing for them to enter his home. Skadi stepped over the threshold of the home and into what any sane person might call a huge mess. The home was in shambles, and trash was strewn all about the place. She kept quiet, but her eyes said more than she could ever verbally.

"I know," said Reginn. "I could stand to tidy up, but . . ."

"Don't worry about it," said Skadi. "Thank you for helping us."

"How long has it been?" said Mimir.

"Too long," said Reginn. "Almost two hundred years."

"I think we last saw one another right after the end of the war. You were a lot younger then."

"Dwarves don't quite have the lifespans of elves or gods, but at least we have the humans beat," said Reginn looking in Skadi's direction. "But I'm reaching the end of my rope. I reckon my days are severely numbered, and I haven't much to live for anyway."

"All of our days are numbered. The early signs of Fimbulwinter are showing," said Mimir.

"The Great Winter?" said Reginn.

"I would nod, but . . ." said Mimir.

"Then what have you come to me for? You should be with your families," said Reginn.

"In all likelihood, it is still years off, and we are facing an immediate problem," said Mimir.

"Do you know the town of Fensalir?" said Skadi.

"I think . . . maybe," said Reginn.

"A powerful jötunn has taken the town hostage and is feeding on its children. I must slay it, but it has empowered some people who are standing between me and it," said Skadi. "Mimir says you have a sword that can help me overcome these people."

"A jötunn that feeds specifically on children?" said Reginn.

"Yes," said Skadi.

Skadi watched the dwarf make eye contact with Mimir.

"I will help you," said Reginn. "But I need something from you in return."

"What?" said Skadi.

"Long ago, my brother Fafnir and I had a serious falling out, but as my end draws near, I find myself wanting to resolve things. He fled to Nidavellir, and I have no way of going there, nor could I even make the journey. My body is too frail for the hostile realm it's become. If you could take a message to him, I will give you Ridill," said Reginn.

Skadi stood up.

"We don't have time for a trip to Nidavellir. We've already gone out of our way to come here," she shouted.

"You help me, and I will help you," said Reginn.

Skadi got in Reginn's face and grabbed the elderly dwarf by the collar.

"We don't have time for this," she said.

"Skadi, it's okay. I know where we can get a Bifrost to take us to Nidavellir," said Mimir.

"Mimir, I trusted you," said Skadi.

"And I haven't betrayed that trust. Reginn needs our help, and in exchange, you'll have a sword that can defend against Dáinsleif. If we face

Hovard and Elfr without it, and they get even one hit on you, it's all over. Don't you think preventing that is worth the bit of time it'll take to do this for Reginn?" said Mimir.

"When my son gets to Hlíðarendi and realizes that Eir was killed by Hovard and Elfr, he is going to question whether I will be able to defeat them. This means he will either come back to help me or go back to Fensalir to face the jötunn. If he does either of those things without me, he will be killed. I don't have time to help Reginn; I have to help my son," said Skadi.

"And I understand your concern but remember, you are doing this for more than just your son. There is an entire town of children who are relying on your success," said Mimir.

"My son is my priority," said Skadi, and she slammed her fist on Reginn's desk.

The desk split in two and crumbled inward. Mimir and Reginn were silent.

"I'm sorry," said Skadi.

"It's quite all right," said Reginn.

"We will find your brother," she said. "What do you want us to tell him?"

"Tell him that I love him," said Reginn.

"That's all?" said Skadi.

"That's all he needs to hear," said Reginn.

"We'll be back before dawn," said Mimir. "Have the sword ready."

"Come back with proof that you spoke with him, and the sword is yours," said Reginn.

"Nidavellir is a dangerous place," said Reginn.

"We're a dangerous pair," said Mimir.

Skadi looked at Mimir out the corner of her eyes.

"What?" said Mimir.

"We'll be back," said Skadi and exited the home with Mimir in hand.

Skadi stepped away from the home then stopped. She held up Mimir's head so it was facing hers.

"Where is the Bifrost?" she said.

"Set me down on that boulder over there.".

Skadi did as was asked of her. Right then, Mimir's left eye began to glow. It shined a light on the ground ahead of him. In the light materialized a relic.

"Pick that up," said Mimir.

She did.

"You are holding a Bifrost key. That will summon the bridge. A good friend gave me that. I hoped to return to Asgard one day but there is only enough juice left in it for two more round trips. This is my gift to you," said Mimir.

"Will you be able to return to Asgard another way if we use this now?" said Skadi.

"I will still have one more roundtrip, and if I must, I can find another way," said Mimir.

"But?" said Skadi.

"But it may be unlikely," said Mimir.

"Then I can't use it. We can just take the sword from Reginn. It has to be around his home somewhere," said Skadi.

"No, I want you to have it. I've thought about this for a while. Going to Asgard won't bring me closure for Odin's betrayal. Using it to help Fensalir and your boy is a far greater use," said Mimir.

"Are you sure?" said Skadi.

"Absolutely," said Mimir.

"Thank you," said Skadi. "How does it work?"

"As you age, your connection to the World Tree dwindles. Because humans age faster than most, your connection dwindles quickly. Though I will say, your connection stays purer in childhood than most other species. But that is beside the point. Before you consumed the Yggdrasil root, the Bifrost key would not have worked for you, but now that you are reconnected to the World Tree, the same energy that unites the nine realms now flows through you as well. Your body is channeling energy that is the basis for all that we know. In the same way that you will your body to act, you can summon the Bifrost Bridge. Think of Nidavellir and just summon away," said Mimir.

Skadi turned the key around in her hand, inspecting it. It was a relic, many hundreds, if not thousands of years old.

"Just will it to act like it's an extension of your . . ." said Mimir.

Before he could finish his sentence, a rainbow shone down from the sky to the ground in front of them. It was bright and powerful. It startled Skadi, and she stepped back.

She inspected it then cautiously approached the beam of energy. Slowly, Skadi reached out and touched it. The Bifrost Bridge was warm and mildly electrifying. She took a deep breath and, with Mimir in hand, passed through.

TWENTY-THREE

NIDAVELLIR

Skadi, with Mimir in hand, emerged instantaneously from the rainbow beam, but it took a moment for both of her senses to adjust to the new setting. They were on a hill that overlooked a valley. The sky was black and covered in smoke from the great forges that decorated the landscape.

Skadi walked up to the edge of the hill and scanned the horizon.

"Where do we start?" she said.

"It's simple," said Mimir. "Look there in the middle."

At the center of the valley was the largest forge and, surprisingly, the only one not billowing smoke.

"The inactive forge?" said Skadi.

"That's the one," Mimir said.

"Hey, you," said a deep voice.

Skadi turned around. Standing before her was a dwarf with a long beard, wielding a sharp ax.

"What are you doing here?" said the dwarf.

"Take it easy," said Skadi. "I don't want to hurt you."

"Uhm," said Mimir. "I think that . . ."

"You should not be here, human," said the dwarf before he started running towards her with the ax, prepared for a strike.

Skadi put her fists up, preparing for the dwarf's attack. The little but powerful creature swung its ax, and Skadi went to bat it aside, but something strange happened. She felt it before she realized what it was.

"Skadi, dodge," said Mimir.

She pulled back and spun on her feet to avoid the ax. The dwarf came down with the blade and missed her entirely but hit the ground and cracked solid rock.

"It's as I feared," said Mimir. "The Yggdrasil root you consumed in Midgard only increases your strength in Midgard. In Nidavellir, you are just human. The Bifrost will still pull you back, but you won't have your strength here."

The dwarf pulled the ax from the rock.

"Human, I don't know how you got here, but you better go back now or face my wrath," said the dwarf.

The dwarf charged Skadi a second time, and just as before, she evaded his attack. She didn't have a weapon, and without the Yggdrasil roots, she was aware of their physical differences despite his size. The cracked rock on the ground was evidence of his strength.

"You have to run," said Mimir.

The dwarf started to swing his ax wildly, chopping to and fro to swipe Skadi with a lethal or at least life-threatening blow. She continued to dance around his blade, but she was gambling at this point. It was only a matter of time until one of those strikes connected.

"Skadi, run," shouted Mimir.

She dropped as low as she could go and kicked the dwarf's feet out from under him as he swung down with the ax. He stumbled forward and crashed into the ground. Skadi grabbed the ax and quickly put distance between her and him.

The dwarf picked himself up and shook his head.

"How did you do that?" he said.

"Listen, dwarf. We are not here to cause you or anyone in this realm harm. I'm just here to relay a message to the brother of Reginn," said Skadi.

"The brother of Reginn?" said the dwarf. "You mean Fafnir. Good luck with that."

"What does that mean?" said Mimir.

"Means no one has seen him in years," said the dwarf.

Skadi looked down at Mimir.

"I don't know," he whispered.

"Will you give me back my ax?" said the dwarf.

"Absolutely not. It's mine now," said Skadi.

"Oh, come on. If the guys find out a human bested me, I'll never hear the end of it," said the dwarf.

"You already aren't going to hear the end of it," said another voice behind Skadi.

She turned around and saw two more dwarves approaching. Each held an ax twice the size of the one she had stolen.

"Dvalinn, you let this human get the better of you," said one of the dwarves.

"I told you not to leave this amateur alone, Dain," said the other dwarf.

"You were right, Alvíss," said Dain.

"Guys, it was a fluke," said Dvalinn.

Alvíss and Dain both laughed.

"Look, fellas, we don't want any trouble," said Mimir.

Skadi started backing up, ax in hand, prepared for a fight but hoping for an escape. Dain took out a knife and tossed it to Dvalinn.

"Think you can hold onto that?" said Dain.

"Very funny," replied Dvalinn.

The three dwarves positioned themselves alongside one another in front of Skadi and Mimir.

"Skadi," said Mimir.

"Get them," said Dain.

"Run," shouted Mimir.

Skadi pivoted and took off as fast as she could muster. She leaped over the edge of the cliff face and ran down the mountain towards the valley's base. Strong as they may have been, the dwarves were not fast, and Skadi quickly put distance between herself and them.

Skadi looked back, and she heard Dain whistle. Behind the three dwarves appeared three horses. They grabbed the horses' reins and hopped into the saddles.

"Yah," shouted Dain.

"Skadi, you can't run any faster?" he said.

"I'm going as fast as I can," she shouted.

"They're catching up faster," shouted Mimir.

Dain made the first swipe with his ax. Skadi ducked it, lost her balance, and started tumbling. She quickly regained her composure and changed direction, running parallel to the valley. The three dwarves all rode past her and took wide turns to circle back and follow.

Skadi kept up her pace as best she could, but no matter how fast she ran, she was no horse, and quickly they were on top of her again. Alvíss chopped at her with his ax. Skadi stopped, turned, and blocked with the ax she had stolen from Dvalinn. The dwarven-steel clanged so loudly it made Skadi and Mimir's ears throb, and though Skadi did as best she could, the momentum plus the strength of the dwarf knocked the ax from her hands. It went flying and landed many feet away. The blade lodged in the dirt.

Skadi's hand throbbed. The force of the hit had sent reverberations through the handle that passed into her forearm.

"What are you going to do?" said Mimir. "There's three of them on horseback, and you don't have your powers, and we can't outrun them."

Skadi eyed Alvíss reach back to strike again as his comrades started circling her and Mimir. He came down with his ax just as he had before, but with nothing to block it, Skadi knew Mimir feared the worst. She did too.

"This is it for you, human," shouted Alvíss.

Skadi shifted backward, dropped Mimir, and with both hands grabbed the ax as the dwarf swung at her. She guided the dwarf's powerful momentum downward, causing him to fall from his horse. In his confusion, she stole his ax and, without any hesitation, used the blunt side to knock him unconscious.

Dain and Dvalinn brought their horses to a complete stop. Skadi picked up Mimir and slung the ax over her shoulder.

"We did not come here to start a fight," she shouted.

"Dvalinn, let's go," said Dain.

"But what about Alvíss?" said Dvalinn.

"We need to regroup," said Dain.

The two remaining dwarves turned their horses and disappeared up the hill from which they'd come.

"Impressive," said Mimir.

"Let's find Fafnir and get back to Midgard," said Skadi.

"Directly ahead," said Mimir.

Skadi turned and continued down the cliffside until she hit the base.

"The forge in the middle is where Fafnir should be," said Mimir.

"The only one not burning?" said Skadi.

"It is the biggest," said Mimir.

"And?" said Skadi.

"Reginn and Fafnir are the surviving sons of the Dwarf King Hreið-marr. They are . . . were . . . I'm not so sure anymore . . . very wealthy," said Mimir.

"Then why does their forge not burn?" said Skadi.

"That is a good question," said Mimir.

Skadi walked into the valley towards the massive, darkened forge. Its inactivity was even more apparent, with smaller active forges operating all around it. Skadi kept up her guard for fear of Dain and Dvalinn returning or other onlookers deciding to test the human and the talking head.

"What happened to their father?" said Skadi.

"Killed," said Mimir.

"That's too bad."

"By Fafnir and Reginn."

Skadi stopped and looked at Mimir curiously.

"They killed their father?" said Skadi.

"They did."

"Did he deserve it?" said Skadi.

"No," said Mimir.

Dwarves stared as Skadi and Mimir scurried to the forge. Those stares did not go unnoticed by either of them. Skadi remained on guard and shot glances at some. They would quickly avert their gaze.

"Why then?" said Skadi.

"Because of the cursed gold of Andvari. You see, Fafnir and Reginn had a third brother named Ótr, and Ótr could shapeshift. One day, he had taken on the likeness of an otter. At the same time, Odin, Loki, and Hœnir were passing by. Loki killed the otter, and the three Aesir gods skinned their catch. Later, they presented the otter's skin to Hreiðmarr when they visited his dwelling, but the Dwarf King immediately realized that it was his son that Loki had killed and demanded payment for his loss. Loki went to gather a ransom which was to fill the otter's skin with gold. Loki, being the trickster he is, filled the skin with the cursed gold of Andvari. The curse, of course, is that it would bring death upon any who possessed it," said Mimir.

"I see," said Skadi.

"The Dwarf King and his family were the victims of the gods' actions," said Mimir.

"You sound like you're not a fan of the gods," said Skadi.

"Some less than others. They have their role to play," said Mimir.

The pair arrived at the front door to the castle forge—it was grand, blackened, and very ornate.

"Over there on the ground is a torch," said Mimir.

Skadi hitched the ax to her pelt, grabbed the torch, and dipped it in the flame by the door before entering the massive, dark hall at the entrance to the castle forge. It was just barely illuminated by the torch.

"For dwarves being so small, they like to live large," whispered Skadi.

"Compensating, I suppose," said Mimir.

"Where to?" said Skadi.

"I suspect this hall leads to a stairwell. Fafnir is likely to be by his treasure which would be kept underground," said Mimir.

Skadi walked through the hall. The torch did little to illuminate it beyond their close vicinity. Columns lined the walking path, and at the end was a throne but no stairs.

"What now?" said Skadi.

"Keep looking. Maybe there is a lever somewhere," said Mimir.

Skadi inspected the throne and felt around the armrests for anything that might trigger a door to open or a staircase to appear.

"Why did Loki kill Ótr?" said Skadi as she continued to investigate the throne.

"Why do the gods do anything?" said Mimir. "Because they can."

Skadi touched an indentation on the left side of the throne, and she and Mimir heard stone start sliding. It came from behind the throne, and what was revealed before them was a stairwell leading underground.

"Good work," said Mimir.

Skadi hopped down from the throne and, with the torch outstretched, began the long descent underground. The staircase was incredibly steep and narrow. The ceiling was only high enough for a dwarf or a human huddled over.

"If Fafnir hasn't been seen in a while, I doubt he's expecting visitors, so just be ready for anything when you get to the bottom of this stairwell," said Mimir.

"I'm ready," said Skadi.

"Not all dwarves are like those troublemakers we encountered earlier, but Fafnir could be a different beast altogether," said Mimir.

After what seemed like an endless journey into the deep, dark underground of Nidavellir, Skadi and Mimir reached the bottom of the staircase. There they came upon another grand hall, but immediately Skadi recognized the glimmer of shiny relics flickering in the light of the torch.

She knelt and picked up a small coin. It was carved beautifully and embedded in the center was a gem of extreme value.

"There are giant torches in those columns," said Mimir.

Skadi lit them and flooded the room with light. All around them was gold and gems. It was a treasure that climbed to the very tall ceilings of the massive hall.

"Andvari's gold," said Mimir.

"I thought you said it was just enough to fill an otter's skin?" said Skadi.

"In the beginning, it was. But included in that cursed gift was Andvaranaut. It is a magic ring that produces gold. It is what made Andvari wealthy and what made Fafnir even wealthier," said Mimir.

A clear path cut through the room. On either side were piles of gold and gems. Skadi and Mimir made their way through, lighting new torches as they progressed. Every time they reached a new torch and thought they'd exhausted the piles of gold, they were greeted by more. Fafnir's treasure had to be the greatest in the nine realms.

"Mimir, how is it you know so much about Midgard and the nine realms if you have been a disembodied head for so long?" said Skadi.

"Just because I am a head does not mean I do not see what has been happening. I told you earlier that even Odin paid a price for my consult. He gave up an eye, an eye that I now use to see through the eyes of his ravens Hugin and Munin."

"You see from the perspective of Odin?" said Skadi.

"No, just his ravens, but they are constantly gathering information for the Allfather and, by extension, me as well," said Mimir.

"Then can you tell me where my son is? Did he make it to Hlíðarendi?" said Skadi.

Mimir closed his eyes. Skadi observed the motion under his eyelids.

Without opening his eyes, Mimir said, "He is there now. A young woman has healed his broken leg. They are talking."

"What about?" said Skadi.

"I only received Odin's eye, not his ears," said Mimir. "She is getting on the horse with him."

"Who is she?" said Skadi.

"Eir shelved her responsibilities as a Valkyrie for the same reason you left your clan," said Mimir.

"She's Eir's daughter?" said Skadi.

"And it seems she intends to help your boy. They are riding towards Fensalir."

"Then we are running out of time. We need to find Fafnir now," said Skadi.

"If he isn't here amongst his treasure, I'm not quite sure where he'd be?" said Mimir.

"Fafnir," shouted Skadi. "Where are you? Your brother sent us."

"Look at what you have found," said a familiar voice.

Skadi turned around and facing her were Dvalinn and Dain. Behind them were five more dwarves. All seven were wielding sharp, giant axes.

"This isn't good," said Mimir.

"You think?" said Skadi.

"What are you going to do?" said Mimir.

"Run," said Skadi.

She pivoted and took off through the gold-filled hall. With every step they took, she could hear the seven dwarves chasing after her. Skadi knew from experience she was faster than them, but that wouldn't matter with the end of the hall fast approaching.

Skadi hit the wall and turned around. The seven dwarves were quickly moving in. She looked left. There was nothing. She looked right. Nothing there either.

"There's writing on this wall," said Mimir. "It's a puzzle. I think it's a doorway."

"Can you solve it?" said Skadi.

"Set me down so I can analyze it," said Mimir.

"Hurry up," said Skadi placing Mimir on top of a pile of gold.

The seven dwarves reached Skadi and stopped only feet away. She unhitched her ax and wielded it in one hand and the torch in the other.

"We knew you were here for the gold," said Dvalinn. "That's why we can't let you live. As soon as we find a way to break Andvari's curse, the gold will enrich Nidavellir in ways you couldn't believe."

"I'm not here for the gold," said Skadi. "I just need to speak with Fafnir."

"I said earlier he hasn't been seen in years," said Dvalinn. "Humans and gods are lying creatures."

"I'm not lying to you," said Skadi.

"Skadi, I almost got it," said Mimir.

"Get her," said Dain.

The seven dwarves charged, and Dvalinn reached her first. He struck with his ax, and Skadi deflected but the force with which he hit was immense and she knew this would be quickly over if Mimir didn't solve the puzzle. Dvalinn struck again, and again she deflected. Dain followed up with a swipe from his ax. Skadi chose to evade then counter. He blocked her counter. A third dwarf came after Dain with a powerful thrust of his ax. Skadi met him with her torch. He stumbled back, patting his face.

"I got it," shouted Mimir. "You're going to have to do what I say."

Skadi deflected Dain and Dvalinn, then another dwarf before having a chance to turn around.

"What?" she shouted.

"With your hand, trace two parallel lines on the wall," said Mimir. "Then from the tops of those two lines connect a third line but in the shape of a V."

Skadi did as she was instructed and drew the first two lines. To her surprise, they left a mark on the wall despite her simply touching it. She then had to quickly evade a strike from one of the dwarves, deflect another and push the torch into another's face. Afterwards, she connected the lines with the V.

"Now connect the lines with an inverted V," said Mimir.

Skadi went to trace her hand against the wall but first had to duck Dain and kick one of the unnamed dwarves. He caught her foot and pulled her off her balance. She chopped at the dwarf with her ax and took his hand. The little creature yelled out, grasping at his nub spewing blood.

"Come on, Skadi," shouted Mimir.

She turned around again and connected the inverted V.

"Now an X through the left line and the right," said Mimir.

Skadi drew the X, then Dvalinn grabbed her hand, and she dropped the torch. His grip was powerful, and despite her best attempt at wrestling her arm free, she could not.

"Now," shouted Dvalinn.

In the flickering light of the torch, Skadi spied Dain running at her with his ax held high. She pulled one last time but couldn't break Dvalinn's grip. Skad jumped and wrapped her legs around the dwarf's neck. The move brought the creature to the ground and caused Dain to trip over him. Dvalinn let Skadi free, and she jumped to finish the markings on the wall. She traced the line, and as soon as she finished, Skadi grabbed Mimir, and the two vanished.

"Where are we?" said Skadi.

"We found Fafnir," said Mimir.

A large torch was burning along the wall to the right. Directly in front of Skadi and Mimir were the skeletal remains of a dwarf wrapped in a beautiful cloak.

"Is this him?" said Skadi.

"My gut, if I had a gut, would tell me yes," said Mimir.

Skadi approached the skeleton. In its right hand was a gold ring. She started to reach for it.

"I wouldn't," said Mimir. "You don't want this curse transferred to you. That's Andvaranaut."

"What do we do then?" said Skadi.

"We fulfill our mission. Tell him," said Mimir.

Skadi approached the skeleton.

"Fafnir," she said. "Your brother loves you."

Mimir and Skadi stood in silence.

"That was a tad anticlimactic," said Mimir.

Then the ring started to glow, and a dark spirit burst forth from it before dissipating just as quickly as it had appeared.

"Oh wow," said Mimir.

"What was that?" said Skadi.

"That was the curse," said Mimir.

Skadi grabbed the ring, and it dripped a droplet of gold into her hand.

"The curse was cast in hate, and most spells are undone by the opposite emotion or action. Just like the runic symbol you drew on the door was a prisoner bind, drawing the opposite will set us free," said Mimir.

"Did Fafnir know this? Why would he bind himself with a spell that could be so easily undone?" said Skadi.

"Well, hardly anyone knows that, but even if he did, Fafnir was illiterate," said Mimir. "He wouldn't have known what to draw anyway."

"Then who did?"

"We did," said Dain, Dvalinn, and the five other dwarves as they materialized before Skadi and Mimir.

"The curse is lifted," shouted Mimir.

"What?" said Dain.

"Just now. We lifted it," said Mimir.

"How?" said Dvalinn.

"The curse was cast in hate, but Fafnir's brother loved him. He genuinely loved him, and that lifted the curse," said Mimir.

Skadi moved to grab Andvaranaut, and the seven dwarves all lunged forward. She stopped.

"I'm going to give you the ring," said Skadi. "If it was cursed and I took the ring into my possession, the curse would transfer to me. Isn't that right, Mimir?"

"That is correct," said Mimir.

"If it isn't cursed and I try to keep it, the seven of you will surely overpower me," said Skadi.

"That is true," said Dvalinn.

"Then I will pick it up, and I will hand it to you," said Skadi.

She started to again reach for the ring. The seven dwarves reacted but eased their tension. Skadi took the ring into her hand and then presented it to Dvalinn. The seven dwarves marveled at the ring before Dvalinn worked up the courage to take it.

"The curse really is lifted," said Dain.

"Will you let us leave here?" said Mimir.

"Who are you two?" said Dvalinn.

"My name is Mimir, wisest man alive," said Mimir.

"And I am Skadi Hervor," said Skadi.

"Well, Mimir and Skadi, Nidavellir is indebted to you both. This ring will provide funding for a lot of fixes that we just could not afford. I am sorry for how we treated you but the last human to journey here was not so kind to our people," said Dain. "We had to be cautious."

"We understand," said Skadi.

"We do?" said Mimir.

"We do," said Skadi.

Dain traced the opposite rune on the wall, and everyone disappeared from within the chamber and reappeared amongst the mounds of gold.

"What happened here?" said Skadi.

"Many years ago, Fafnir arrived back in his home of Nidavellir, having just killed his father, our king. For a long time afterward, he was cruel, but eventually, he became aware of the curse and asked to be sealed away with the source of the curse so that it would die with him. He trusted us, his father's and his' guard to make sure he never saw the light of day again," said Dain.

"We didn't know how to break the curse, and we knew that by sealing him off, we were also sealing off our only chance at ever revitalizing our realm. That was until now," said Dvalinn.

"Will one of you travel with us to Midgard to tell Reginn we conveyed his message to his brother?" said Mimir.

"I will. Not only for you, but he needs to come back to Nidavellir. He is heir to the throne," said Dvalinn.

"Thank you," said Mimir.

Reginn sat in front of his fireplace, quietly embracing the warmth and silence, when a loud crash sounded outside his door. All the colors of the rainbow flooded through his windows, decorating his entire, modest house. He shot up and ran to the door.

Standing outside the home was Skadi holding Mimir and a dwarf he had not seen in many years.

"Dvalinn?" said Reginn.

"Reginn," said Dvalinn.

"It is good to see you, but what are you doing here?" said Reginn.

"Hi, old friend. I'm here on behalf of these two," said Dvalinn.

"We relayed your message to your brother," said Mimir. "But . . ."

"But what?" said Reginn.

"Your brother has passed on," said Skadi.

"It's true," said Dvalinn.

Reginn sighed and shook his head. He wiped a single tear from his eyes then walked back into his house. Skadi and Dvalinn stood there in the doorway while Reginn rummaged around his home. He soon returned, holding a sheathed sword.

"This is Ridill," he said, handing it to Skadi. "It is one of the finest weapons in the nine realms, made from dwarven steel and strengthened with power runes in the hilt. If this won't help you win against whom you're fighting, then run away because you're fighting Odin."

Reginn watched with pride as Skadi took the weapon and unsheathed it. It shimmered and was lightweight but still had some heft to it.

"Thank you," she said and slipped the sword away.

"Reginn, there is something I must ask of you," said Dvalinn.

"What is it?" Reginn said, wiping a second tear.

"Nidavellir is on the cusp of a radical transformation. Will you lead us?" said Dvalinn.

"You want me to take the throne?" said Reginn. "Am I fit to be king?"

"I believe you are," said Dvalinn.

"As do I," said Mimir.

"It's just I haven't been home in so long," said Reginn.

He shifted his attention to Skadi when she put a hand on his shoulder.

"We all have reservations when we find out who or what we are supposed to be, but the strength to lead or to do what is right comes from within. It comes from here," said Skadi pointing at Reginn's heart. "Answering the call to action is not something you can typically prepare for but answering it for the right reason will help guide you."

The dwarf took Skadi's hand in his and held it tight.

"Thank you," he said.

"If we are done here, Skadi and I must finish our mission," said Mimir. "We'll drop you both off in Nidavellir, then be on our way."

"Let's go," said Reginn.

"You don't need to grab anything?" said Dvalinn.

"No. This was never meant to be my home," said Reginn. "I have nothing here."

"All right then," said Mimir. "Skadi, if you will do us the honors."

She held out the Bifrost key. The rainbow bridge appeared before them. Reginn followed Dvalinn towards it. Upon reaching it, Reginn turned around.

"Be careful, you two. I once heard of a jötunn that eats children. I don't remember the particulars, but I do remember it having something to do with the Aesir gods," said Reginn.

"Thanks for the warning," said Skadi.

Reginn nodded then he and Dvalinn passed through to Nidavellir. The rainbow bridge closed, and Mimir disappeared the Bifrost within his eye from whence it had come.

"You no longer have any round trips left in this thing," said Skadi.

"I know."

"Are you okay with that?"

"I decided to help, just like I am helping you. And I would make the same decision again."

"No blood oath for them, though," said Skadi.

Mimir smiled.

"Maybe I am growing too."

TWENTY-FOUR

STRONGER TOGETHER

Frija was startled awake when she heard footsteps charging past the entrance to the cave she took refuge.

"The search party," she whispered.

"Is someone going to check that cave?" a voice shouted.

"I'll go," said another.

"You two go with him," another voice shouted.

"Damn it," whispered Frija as she retreated deeper into the cave.

The footsteps were hot on her trail. The blackness of the cave made maneuvering slow for both her and them, but they were catching up. Frija ducked under low-hanging stalactites and around large stalagmites.

"I think I hear something," shouted one of the voices.

"Back here," said another.

She kept moving further into the cave, increasing her pace as best she could without running in the darkness. But the footsteps were right behind her. She could feel the presence of people coming. If something didn't happen soon, they'd be on her.

This search party would not be a problem if she had her runes, but she was just a single person without access to her powers, and she knew she stood little chance against the horde. Jagged rocks scraped her legs and arms. One rock cut her forehead, and blood started dripping into her right eye. If it wasn't already hard enough to see in the darkness, this didn't help. She leaped over a deep ravine and stopped around the corner just out of sight to catch her breath.

"Hey, be careful," one of the voices shouted.

Frija assumed they had arrived at the ravine she'd just cleared.

"No one is back here," said another voice.

"Should we turn around?" said a voice.

"Yea," said one person.

"No one is there, and if she is, then she'll be dead soon enough. This isn't called the Cave of the Dying for no reason," said one of the voices.

"The Cave of the Dying?" whispered Frija.

Just then, the ground beneath her started to crumble and give, and she quickly slipped beneath the surface. Frija fell into a shaft that carried her down into the ravine she had jumped over and crashed into a pile of skeletal remains.

She couldn't see a thing, but she could feel the femurs, ribs, skulls, and other bones that had once belonged to some unfortunate soul who had found themselves in a similar situation to her current predicament. Frija scrambled to gain her footing and put her back against the wall of the ravine. She felt for the opening that she had just fallen through and quickly realized how steep an incline it was.

"I'm stuck," she said.

Alver observed Frija's home from afar. Guards were moving in and out of it, and he could not think of a good enough reason to be there.

"This is a dead end," he whispered.

He turned around and started walking away from the home when one of the search parties crossed his path.

"Hey," said a person in the party.

Alver looked left and right.

"You," said the man. "What are you doing?"

"Nothing," said Alver.

"Wasn't your boy one of the witch's victims? Why aren't you a part of a search party?" said the man.

"I . . . I was just about to help," said Alver.

"Join ours then," said the man.

Alver nodded and merged with the party. In the earliest part of the day, they methodically covered parts of Fensalir. A little later, but still quite early, they arrived at the outskirts of the town near the entrance to an ancient cave most residents didn't even know existed.

"Is someone going to check that cave?" said one woman in the party.

"I'll go," said Alver.

"You two go with him," said another member of the party.

Alver entered the cave with a man and a woman, and the three gingerly maneuvered through the darkness.

"I think I hear something," said the man who was accompanying Alver.

"Back here," said the woman.

They quickened their pace, careful not to injure themselves in the darkness, but they soon had to stop upon arriving at a deep ravine.

"Hey, be careful," the man said.

"No one is back here," said Alver.

"Should we turn around?" said the woman.

"Yea," said Alver.

"No one is there, and if she is, then she'll be dead soon enough. This isn't called is the Cave of the Dying for no reason," said the man.

Alver, the man, and the woman began walking back towards the entrance when they heard the shuffling of feet on the dirt.

"Let's get out of here," said the man. "I don't like the feel of this place."

"Agreed," said the woman.

Alver let them lead so they wouldn't see him looking back at the ravine. Soon they emerged from the cave, and the search party continued. Alver let himself drift to the rear of the party and broke away when he saw an opening. He hid behind a tree until the party was out of sight then ran back to the cave.

When Alver reached the ravine, he leaned over and shouted, "Is someone down there? I'm here to help."

Frija had not given up but was perplexed on how she would escape when Alver shouted down to her. At first, she thought she was hallucinating but quickly realized she was not.

"Should I answer?" she whispered to herself.

149

"Hello," shouted Alver. "Is someone down there?"

"What am I going to do?" Frija whispered.

"I know you think I'm with the search party, but I can assure you I am not. My name is Alver Ketill. I saw the jötunn. I know you aren't the villain they're saying you are."

"Alver Ketill, father of Dofri Ketill?" said Frija.

"That's me," said Alver.

"Alver, if you saw the jötunn, how did you escape?" said Frija.

"It attacked my wife and I back at the council hall. I escaped, but . . ." Alver drifted off.

"I'm sorry," said Frija.

"Are you hurt?" he said.

"Just superficially, but I am stuck. I need a rope to get out of here," said Frija.

"Hang tight. I'll be right back," said Alver.

Alver ran out of the cave and didn't stop until he reached his home. He rummaged through the storage closet in the back and found a bundle of rope.

"What are you doing?" said a guard standing in his doorway.

"I'm . . ." said Alver. "What do you mean?"

"I saw you running. Why aren't you with a search party, and what are you doing with that rope?" said the guard.

"I . . . I . . . I think you are mistaken. I wasn't running anywhere," said Alver.

"You're not a good liar. You're sweating. Now tell me what you're doing, or I will report you to Liótr," said the guard.

The image of Liótr taking to the sky on the undead bird flashed in Alver's mind.

"One of the people in the search party I was just with is stuck in the Cave of the Dying," said Alver. "She fell into the ravine, and I needed a rope to get her out."

"Only fools enter that cave," said the guard.

"We were trying to be thorough. As you know, the witch killed my son," said Alver.

"I am aware," said the guard. "Here, I will come to help you rescue them."

"You don't have to do that," said Alver.

"I will help," said the guard.

"Fine," said Alver. "Right this way."

Alver gestured for the guard to exit, and when the guard turned around, Alver jumped on the man and put him in a chokehold. He cut off the man's oxygen with everything he could muster until he stopped struggling, then gently brought him to the ground. He stuffed the man's mouth with a cloth and bound him up with the rope he'd planned on using to free Frija.

"Now what?" he whispered.

He ran back to the cave, careful not to be seen this time.

"Frija, are you still there?" he asked.

"I am. Did you get the rope?" she asked.

"I had to use it to tie up a guard. Is there no other way to get you free?"

"Do you know Skadi and her son Bjorn Hervor? Do you know where they live?"

"I don't."

"They live near the tree that looks like a dragon. Do you know the one I mean?"

"I do."

"Their home is the only one by it. Skadi has a hjell out back where she dries cod. There will be rope. Be extremely careful. They will be watching their home," said Frija.

"Hang tight. I'll be right back," said Alver.

"I'm not going anywhere," said Frija.

Again, Alver exited the cave and quickly made for the old dragon-shaped tree. He knew the place. He used to play there as a child.

As he approached, he slowed down and took cover. Multiple guards were walking this way and that. If the watch parties weren't enough to be concerned with, Liótr's men were always lurking.

Alver watched the guards move this way and that, going in and out of the home and circling it. They had a pattern, but they also would move sporadically.

"I cannot afford to get caught," he whispered.

He picked up a rock and threw it as hard as he could. It clanged off the right side of the home. The guards that were patrolling all noticed and quickly scurried to check things out. As fast as they ran to the right of the house, Alver ran to the left. The hjell was in sight, and he scurried to the door. He checked left and right then went inside.

Just as Frija had said, there was plenty of rope. Fish dangled from it, and there was enough to get Frija out of the ravine. He quickly started tossing the fish in the corner and wrapping the rope around his arm so it would be easy to transport back to the cave.

"Someone is around here," said one of the guards. "I'll check in here."

Alver heard the man approaching the hjell.

"Shit," he said.

"Hey, what are you doing here?" said the guard.

Alver thought they found him but realized the guard had not entered the hjell and was talking to someone outside of it. Then there was a crash and a bang as the guard bounced off the outside of the fish shed.

"Someone help," said the guard.

There was a scrambling of movement, but it didn't last long. Someone or something was making quick work of the guards patrolling the grounds.

"That about does it," said an unfamiliar voice.

"What now?" asked another unfamiliar voice.

"We keep looking for Frija. She wasn't at her home. I thought she'd be here," said one of the voices.

Alver hurried over to the door of the hjell, paused for a moment, then emerged. Standing before him were Bjorn and Eirdóttir.

"Who are you?" said Bjorn.

"Alver Ketill. I can show you where Frija is," said Alver looking over the guards who were lying around unconscious. "You two did this?"

"What is going on here?" said Bjorn.

"You probably know more than me. You're Skadi's son, right?" said Alver.

"I am. How do you know me?" said Bjorn.

152

"Frija sent me here to get a rope from your mother's hjell. Frija is stuck. You two can help me get her free if we can sneak past the guards and the watch parties covering the town," said Alver.

Just then, there was a loud caw overhead. Alver, Bjorn, and Eirdóttir looked up and saw an enormous bird, and on its back were two people.

"Get inside," said Alver pushing Bjorn and Eirdóttir into the hjell.

"What is that?" said Eirdóttir.

"That's two of the council members," said Alver. "They've been patrolling from the sky since yesterday. Everyone is looking for Frija. She's been blamed for all the dead children, including my son, but I know it isn't her. I met the jötunn at the council hall after it . . . after it killed my wife."

"I'm sorry," said Bjorn.

"A lot has happened recently. The council members manipulated Buna . . . well, not just Buna . . . they convinced me too that it was the right thing to do."

"The right thing to do what?" said Bjorn.

"To put Frija on the defensive. Apparently, Frija's powers are linked to the runes in her home, but because Frija is confined to Fensalir for some reason, the council members voted to redraw the lines of the town, so it did not include Frija's home. They needed a quorum for the vote, hence getting my wife," said Alver.

"Frija is not the monster," said Eirdóttir. "My mother and her were close."

"I know," said Alver. "That is why we need to rescue her, but with those council members overhead, we are in a tricky predicament."

"If we must, the two of us can handle a fight, but let's not use that as option A," said Eirdóttir.

Alver peaked outside of the hjell and looked up. The undead bird and its passengers were circling back.

"Where is your mother?" said Alver. "She would be helpful in this situation."

"I don't know," said Bjorn. "We had to split up. I'm not sure if she is going to make it back to help with the coming fight."

"I'm sorry I asked," said Alver.

He peaked up at the sky again. The undead bird and its passengers passed by, and on they continued. Alver watched until he was confident, they were not turning around, then gestured for Bjorn and Eirdóttir to scurry out of the hjell.

"This way," he said. "Follow me."

"Wait," said Bjorn.

"What?" Alver said.

"I need to grab another bow from the house," said Bjorn.

The three snuck through Fensalir, careful not to be seen by any of the numerous search parties scouring the town. Alver led, followed by Eirdóttir, with Bjorn bringing up the rear. At a modest pace, they made good time and were at the Cave of the Dying shortly after leaving Skadi and Bjorn's home.

"Frija," said Alver as they approached the ravine.

"Still here," said Frija.

Alver prepared to throw the rope over the ravine's edge, but Eirdóttir grabbed his hand and stopped him.

"I'll handle it," she said.

Alver looked at her curiously, then jumped back when she sprouted wings from her back.

"A Valkyrie," he said.

He watched with astonishment as she leaped into the ravine, and moments later, reappeared with Frija in her arms. The two women landed, and the wings disappeared.

"My mother was a Valkyrie," said Eirdóttir.

Alver's amazement continued as he observed Eirdóttir grab Frija's arm and quickly healed all her scrapes and cuts from having been pursued through the cave in the dark.

"Thank you," said Frija.

"I found these two when I went to Skadi's home," said Alver.

"Bjorn, where is your mother?" said Frija.

"We were ambushed shortly after getting the second root by one of the council members and mom's uncle, Hovard Hervor. We escaped, but mom was afraid it would be too much for me and sent me back to Hlíðarendi. However, when I got to Hlíðarendi, I learned that Hovard and the council member killed . . . Eirdóttir's mother, and I wasn't sure my mom would succeed. I met Eirdóttir, and she offered to help, so we came back to stop the jötunn ourselves," said Bjorn.

"Eir was killed?" said Frija. "I am sorry for your loss, Eirdóttir. I never meant for anything to happen to her. She was just supposed to introduce Skadi to Gunnar. The price for this journey is high."

"My mother did what she did, knowing the risk."

"Frija, you set us on this course. What happens next?" said Bjorn.

"I sought out Skadi because I had a vision that she would be the solution to the madness here in Fensalir, but like all visions, it was not clear as to the exact path she would have to take. All I knew was that she would need the roots of the Yggdrasil to do it. But, even as vague as they may be, visions do not always come to pass, or they sometimes happen in ways truly unforeseen. For example, I always knew Eir would pass, but years from now during Ragnarök, not against Hovard. Therefore, I cannot tell you the exact next steps, nor can I tell you if your mother will be successful against her uncle. But I can strategize. Between the three of us . . ." said Frija.

Alver cleared his throat.

"Four of us," said Frija. "I think we can outmaneuver the jötunn and save Fensalir. Bjorn, you consumed the Yggdrasil roots, correct?"

"Two of them," said Bjorn.

"And Eirdóttir, you have all the powers of a Valkyrie, right?" said Frija.

"I do," said Eirdóttir.

"And Alver, you spent your whole life in Fensalir. You know the ins and outs of this town better than any of us. Am I right?" said Frija.

"Yes," said Alver.

"This sounds like the making of a promising team," said Frija.

TWENTY-FIVE

DEATH

"Finish the story of Kvasir," said Skadi as she ran through the woods towards Mímisbrunnr.

"Begrudgingly, I admit that Kvasir was the wisest of all beings in the nine realms. You could ask this man a question about anything, and he would have an answer. One day he decided he would become a wanderer and dispense knowledge across the realms. He went everywhere for years. But his journey came to an end when he met two dwarves named Fjalar and Galar. Despite Kvasir's great wisdom, the two dwarves tricked him into letting down his guard, and they killed him. They drained his blood and mixed it with honey to make the Mead of Poetry," said Mimir.

"Earlier, you said you had been exchanged for Kvasir, but if he was created at the end of Aesir-Vanir War by the Aesir and the Vanir, then how is that possible?"

"The man I was traded for was not Kvasir but Loki. I lied, and I'm sorry, but I try to limit my association to the Trickster God. Reference to Loki is usually a bit distracting. During the war, he had found himself imprisoned by the Vanir, and the Aesir wanted him back despite his tricks," said Mimir.

"Twice now, I've heard of Loki's exploits. How dangerous is he?" said Skadi.

"Extremely."

"Do not lie again."

"I am sorry I lied about whom I was traded for. I didn't want you associating me with Loki. He is a plague and someone to watch out for if you ever cross his path," said Mimir.

Bjorn and Alver evaded two watch parties as they made for a wooden structure near Sökkvabekkr Swamp. Alver led, and Bjorn kept them safe.

"There it is," said Alver.

The two approached cautiously.

"If the runes are anywhere, this is a good place to start. Most of the killings have happened near the swamp, and we were here when we caught wind of our son, so it must be the home of the jötunn," said Alver.

"I should probably go first then," said Bjorn.

Bjorn slowly walked up to the tiny structure while Alver stayed close behind. He reached out and grabbed the handle. Despite the locked door, Bjorn broke the handle with just a small exertion of force, and the door creaked open. A cold burst of air washed over him. Bjorn looked back at Alver then the two proceeded to enter.

The inside of the structure was dark, but Bjorn could see the hole in the ground. He inched towards it and could feel the cold air originating from underground as he peeked over the edge.

"How far down do you think it goes?" said Alver.

"Only one way to find out," said Bjorn. "Do you want to stay here?"

"No," said Alver. "I'm coming with you."

Bjorn hesitated, then nodded and led them underground.

Once the pair reached the bottom of the hole, Bjorn and Alver were in total darkness. The cold was even more severe. It pierced their pelts as they slowly began navigating the pitch-black corridor.

Bjorn accepted a small torch from Alver, who had just lit up two for them to light their way.

"If we get caught down here, that may be it for us," said Alver.

"That's what I'm here for," said Bjorn.

"But you only ate two of the three roots, did you not?" said Alver.

"That's two more than you," said Bjorn.

"This isn't a joke. If we get caught down here, we will have a problem," said Alver.

157

"I know," said Bjorn. "I understand."

After a minute of walking, the pair arrived at a fork in the road.

"So, where do you think Frija's runes would be if they were kept underground?" said Bjorn.

"Somewhere central," said Alver. "A place the jötunn could access easily if it needed to."

"And where might that be?" said Bjorn.

"We entered the shed above facing north towards Himinbjorg Mountain, which means that Fensalir proper is south of where we are standing. The most central place in Fensalir is the council hall building. If we take the left corridor, then we should be heading in the correct direction," said Alver.

"Left it is," said Bjorn.

While Bjorn and Alver were trekking underground, Frija and Eirdóttir were just as busy above ground.

Eirdóttir landed at the mouth of the Cave of the Dying, and her wings retracted and disappeared.

"They're flying a pattern," said Eirdóttir. "They crisscross Fensalir, then do a wide circle before crisscrossing again."

"Okay, good. So, we know where they are and where they're likely to be. We also know that watch parties are scouring the town, and Elfr is with Hovard Hervor outside Fensalir. What we don't know is where Dana Robert or the jötunn are," said Frija.

"How can we find them?" said Eirdóttir.

"We have to smoke them out," said Frija. "We need to pick each individual off one by one, saving the jötunn for last if possible. Liótr has super strength, and Lofn can summon the dead. Elfr has the power to control the minds of lesser beings. Hovard has elemental control over fire, but Dana, the council president, is unknown. I never saw her use her power. Whatever it is, it's powerful because I know the others still respect her. We will need to know what she can do before we go after her. But first, we need to find her."

"If Bjorn and Alver can find your runes, it'll be a whole lot easier," said Eirdóttir.

"If is the big question. I know the jötunn collected them, but I also know the jötunn can't use them, so I at least need to know what he plans for them," said Frija. "While they work on that, though, you and I can figure out the distraction to draw out Dana and the jötunn."

"Where is the council hall?" said Eirdóttir.

"In the center of town," said Frija.

"Do you think we can draw them out there?"

"I lit the place on fire yesterday and didn't see her. We need another approach," said Frija.

Eirdóttir scratched her chin.

"I got it," she said.

Dana was sitting at home with her feet propped up on her desk, going over some documents pertaining to the town, when a knock at her front door caught her attention.

"What is it?" she said.

"Ma'am, I have something I think you should see," said the guard at the door.

Dana got up, walked over to the door, and opened it.

The guard was holding a sheet of paper. Dana took it and scanned it over.

"Where did you find this?" she said.

"It's all over," said the guard.

"All over where?" said Dana.

"All over Fensalir," said the guard.

Dana crumbled the paper and threw it to the ground.

"Shit," she said.

The gathering outside the remains of the council hall was a madhouse. All the search parties had gathered there. Hundreds of people were shouting obscenities and holding up the same piece of paper that Dana saw.

As she approached, the guard that had arrived at her door took the lead and parted the sea of people.

"You lied to us," shouted another person.

"Back up. Back all the way up," shouted the guard.

"We trusted you," shouted someone.

"Those are our kids you killed," shouted an anonymous person.

Dana maneuvered the crowd, sticking close to the guard, ignoring the taunts from the mob until she reached what was left of the council hall building. She then turned to address everyone.

"Listen up," she said.

The crowd died down a bit.

"I said listen up," she shouted.

The crowd grew silent.

"This is a lie," she said, holding up the paper. "The person who is distributing these just wants to distract you from the true culprit. It is probably the witch herself."

"It says you conspired with a jötunn," shouted someone in the crowd. "It says you all did."

"That's not true," said Dana.

"A jötunn makes more sense than a witch," shouted someone else. "I've never heard of a witch eating children, but I have heard of a jötunn that does."

"Yeah, me too," shouted another.

"Same here," shouted another after that.

"Listen, everyone," said Dana. "This is exactly the kind of deception a witch would participate in. If we are turning on each other, then she is winning. We need to keep focused on the true perpetrator."

"But what about that bird that keeps flying overhead? Where did that come from?" shouted someone.

"We asked the gods for air assistance, and they felt so inclined to grant it. Liótr and Lofn are up there patrolling for the witch," said Dana.

"We want answers," shouted a person in the crowd. "What is really going on here in Fensalir?"

"What is going on is that we have a witch problem," said Dana, patience starting to wane. "We all know that Midgard is a hard place to live and that towns are a way for humans to stave off the creatures that would have us for lunch. But despite our best efforts, one of those creatures has snuck into our town, and we need to stick together to root her out. If we are fighting each other, then we are all doomed. Whoever put these signs up knows that. It's divide and conquer tactics."

"How can we trust you?" shouted a person in the crowd. "These killings have been going on for so long. What's different now?"

"I can't give you a reason for the killings lasting as long as they have. That is a failure on our part as this town's leadership, but I can assure you that we are committed to bringing them to an end. If you reorganize into watch parties, we can bring this witch to justice. Fensalir is not a big town, though it is expansive, but her hiding places exponentially shrinks when we organize. It is only a matter of time until we find her," said Dana.

"She has a point," shouted someone.

"The more we stand around, the longer the witch remains uncaught," shouted someone else.

Standing by herself in the middle of the crowd, watching the mob descend on Dana then begin to refocus on Frija, was Eirdóttir. She was holding one of the signs she had put up around town.

"Now to find the jötunn," she whispered.

"We've been walking for almost an hour," said Bjorn. "How much further do you think?"

"Shouldn't be long now. We are really deep underground," said Alver.

"I suspected so," said Bjorn. "We've been on a steady decline ever since we started in this direction."

Alver continued to follow as they crept along in the dark. The passageway they were on had twisted but never so much that it changed their overall direction, but it had grown more confined, and the claustrophobia it induced in both was very real. The cold, too, was wearing them down. A steady breeze had brushed over them the entire time they'd been underground, and despite the heavy pelts they each wore, they were freezing.

The passage then came to an end and opened into a large cavern. For the first time, since they'd gone underground, Bjorn and Alver could stand apart from one another and upright. The cold was still there, but at least they had some breathing room.

"I think this is it," said Alver. "We should be under the council hall."

"Okay, let's fan out and start searching this place. If the runes are here, we must find them," said Bjorn.

The two split up. Bjorn took the left side of the cavern and Alver, the right. With their torches, they carefully scanned over their respective territories.

Alver walked along the wall of the cavern, using it to trace his steps. He held the torch far above his above his head. He moved slowly, paying extra close attention to the ground immediately ahead of him. But, despite his attentiveness, he stepped on something that cracked. The sound of the crunch caught his attention more than the slight pain that shot up through his foot.

"What was that?" said Bjorn.

Alver looked down and moved his foot back. At first, it didn't register what it was; then, after his brain had a second to process it, he realized he had stepped on a bone. He knelt and grabbed it to inspect it with the light of the torch. Bjorn ran over to stand by him.

"Oh my," whispered Alver.

"That's human," said Bjorn.

"Not every child was found," said Alver. "More times than not, we never found a body; the child would simply be assumed missing."

Alver watched Bjorn lift his torch high overhead and walk forward, soon coming upon a pile of femurs, ribs, and skulls as tall as himself.

"The jötunn was bringing them here," said Bjorn.

Alver gulped.

"This is his home," he said.

"There must be at least forty skeletons down here," said Bjorn.

"How long has this been going on?" said Alver rhetorically.

From the sky, Liótr and Lofn spied the mass demonstration that had formed at the council hall.

"What do you think that's all about?" said Lofn.

"No idea," said Liótr.

Lofn grabbed her head and massaged her temples.

"What is it?" Liótr said

"The dead are speaking to me," she said.

"What are they saying?" said Liótr.

"Skadi's boy Bjorn and Buna's husband Alver have found his feeding ground," said Lofn.

"This isn't good," said Liótr. "If they expose what's really been happening here, we are all finished. Where is the damn jötunn?"

Lofn let go of her head and looked down once again at the demonstration.

"I told you this does not end well," she whispered.

While Alver and Bjorn searched the cavern deep under Fensalir, and Eirdóttir stood in the crowd keeping tabs on Dana, Frija was busy working on a way to draw out the jötunn. Little did she know, she would not need a plan.

"Where could this damn beast have gotten to?" she said to herself.

"I'm here," said the jötunn.

Frija turned around, and standing before her was the unhuman, child-killing beast in the flesh.

"How did you find me?" said Frija.

"Your halfling Valkyrie placed those signs in a pattern that was more tightly dispersed near the Cave of the Dying, which led me to believe she originated here, and so I thought I would check it out myself. The humans were proving themselves ineffective, but I'm sure you are familiar with their shortcomings," said the jötunn.

The jötunn stepped forward. Frija stepped backward.

"Severed from your power and stripped of your runes . . . that pretty much makes you human. Am I right?" said the jötunn.

"You're a coward who feeds on the weakest in Midgard. If you were really a threat, you'd go after the big fish in Asgard," said Frija.

The jötunn took another step forward, and Frija took another step backward.

"Is that what you think I'm doing? Is that why you think I choose human children? Frija, you have me mistaken. No. Human children are pure. Their energy and lifeblood aren't tainted by the decisions we creatures of the nine realms make regularly. Humans have the shortest lifespan of all the creatures of the nine realms, so their children are the purest. Have you ever seen a troll child? Childhood for a troll is fifty years. A fifty-year-old anything is a sour being," said the jötunn. "Sure, maybe I could go after an infant troll, but there are far more humans, and to be honest . . . why risk it when humans are so weak . . . mentally and physically."

"What do you need all of this for?" said Frija.

"To survive Ragnarök," said the jötunn. "Surely you have seen the signs of Fimbulwinter approaching?"

"I have," said Frija.

"Then you understand," said the jötunn. "I needed a place I could feed uninterrupted."

The jötunn stepped forward again. It was practically on top of Frija. She pivoted to run, but it grabbed her by the arm and yanked her back around.

"Your meddling is over. You're done," said the jötunn.

"I'm not afraid to die," said Frija.

"I know you aren't. You have always had my respect Frija. I admired your defiance of Aesir all those years ago, but you are in my way now and that I cannot allow."

"When Skadi returns, you will meet a swift end. I have foreseen it," said Frija.

"Your attack dog. How well do you think she'll fair when her handler is no longer here to direct her?" said the jötunn.

"Well enough," said Frija.

The jötunn scowled and grabbed Frija by the neck, lifting her off the ground. She fought his grasp but to no avail.

"No rune or champion to help you and no place to run," said the jötunn before snapping Frija's neck.

Her limp body hit the ground and rolled to a stop with her face in the dirt.

The jötunn glanced upward and smirked.

Simultaneously Mimir, Lofn, and Eirdóttir all knew that Frija was dead.

TWENTY-SIX

BLACK SMOKE RISING

Elfr sat on a boulder by the well at Mímisbrunnr. In his hand, he toyed with Dáinsleif. Across from him, by smoldering embers, was Hovard. He, too, sat in silence, waiting. The world troll loomed over both, casting them in its shadow.

"What do you have against Skadi?" said Elfr.

Elfr got Hovard's attention and met his gaze.

"I was enjoying the quiet," he said.

Elfr stood up and sheathed the sword. He walked over to the smoldering embers and sat down.

"Tell me," he said. "Full disclosure, I have been trying to read your mind for a while now, and I can't crack it. I suspect the jötunn knows what you want because I'm sure he would not have granted you those gifts if he didn't but enlighten me. I'm curious. I want to know."

Hovard got up and walked away. Elfr followed.

"Come on," said Elfr. "What is it?"

"We have a working relationship. I'm not here for a friend or confidant. You don't need to know me, and I don't care about you," said Hovard.

"Are you still mad about those guys at Hlíðarendi? I thought we worked that out?" said Elfr.

"That does not mean we are friends," said Hovard.

Elfr rolled his eyes and turned away from Hovard. He walked back to the fire and stopped dead in his tracks. Standing at the edge of the forest that surrounded their campsite was Skadi. She wielded an ax in one hand and a mighty broadsword in the other.

"Hovard," shouted Elfr.

Moments Earlier:

"Slow down," said Mimir. "We are fast approaching."

Skadi came to a stop.

"Mímisbrunnr is just up ahead. I know we have the dwarven sword now, but maybe we should devise a plan?" he said.

"I have a plan. I'm going to kill them," said Skadi.

"Yeah, I think we should definitely devise a plan," said Mimir.

"What are you thinking?" said Skadi.

"The world troll and Dáinsleif are what make Elfr dangerous, but without those things, he is just a man. Hovard, however, is dangerous himself and therefore the primary obstacle."

"I know this," said Skadi.

"Let's think about your strengths for a second. You're fast, you're strong, you're durable, you're an experienced fighter, and you have a high-quality weapon. You also have me to watch your back so you can see in multiple directions at once," said Mimir.

"Those things can all be said about our opponents," said Skadi.

"At best, we are at a stalemate," said Mimir.

"We're not at a stalemate because we do have one advantage. People to fight for," said Skadi.

"People to fight for," said Mimir with a smile. "Not exactly the plan I was thinking of, but motivation can be the deciding factor in battles. When you get out there, go for the world troll's head as soon as possible, then focus on Hovard. I'll make sure Elfr doesn't get close, and if he does, that is what Ridill is for," said Mimir.

Present:

"What?" said Hovard rushing to see what it was about that Elfr had been shouting.

He saw her as soon as he turned the corner.

"Skadi," said Hovard.

"Nice sword," said Elfr. "Is that what took you so long to get here? Won't do you any good against mine."

He drew Dáinsleif.

"What's that on your back," said Hovard noticing a harness.

"Shouldn't have thrown me away," shouted Mimir.

"You survived," said Hovard.

"You'll wish I hadn't," shouted Mimir.

Skadi raised her sword and ax into a combative stance.

Elfr smirked.

The ground trembled as the world troll started to move. Skadi felt the Midgardian soil shift under her feet as the massive creature stirred to life. At the same time, Hovard formed flames around his hands.

"Crush them," shouted Elfr, arm outstretched and pointed in Skadi's direction.

The world troll swooped in with its right hand clenched into a massive, human-sized fist. Skadi leaped into the air, and the fist crossed beneath her. She landed on its wrist and started running up the monster's forearm. The world troll tried to shake her off. She lost her footing but caught herself by stabbing Ridill deep into the creature's arm and used her momentum to bring herself upright again. She continued the charge up the world troll's arm, but a blast of fire from Hovard stopped in her tracks. She leaped backward to avoid the fire that would have cooked her instantly. The world troll was not so lucky, and Hovard seared its flesh with the powerful flames. The beast let out a yell so powerful that all the birds in the surrounding trees took flight.

The creature grabbed its burnt flesh with its left hand, then swiped at Skadi, who was ascending its right bicep. She jumped and dodged the creature.

"You're doing it," shouted Mimir.

Skadi continued up to the creature's shoulder, but Hovard landed in front of her, immediately intercepting her path. He shot a blast of fire at her so bright and powerful the world troll had to avert its gaze. Skadi dropped to the side of the creature's arm and hooked herself in with the ax she wielded and Ridill. Hovard followed her but used the flames he emitted from his palms to fly down. The world troll twisted its arm, so he had a clear shot.

"Move," shouted Mimir.

Hovard's flames came rocketing towards Skadi. She pulled her weapons free and dropped to the ground, landing with such force that the ground cratered around her.

Elfr was already on top of her and swung with Dáinsleif. Skadi blocked with the ax, but his sword cut the ax's blade in two, rendering the weapon useless.

"Ridill," shouted Mimir.

Elfr kept up the assault and went for Skadi's abdomen, but she blocked with Ridill, and the clang of the two swords sent shockwaves across the battlefield.

"Stay back," shouted Hovard.

Skadi tried to stop Elfr's retreat but quickly dodged as Hovard rained fire. Her pelt caught some of the flames and was burning. She patted it out and turned on the world troll again.

Skadi leaped at the creature's chest. The world troll swiped at her. She jabbed the sword in its hand and used its momentum against it. Ridill passed through the creature's palm and projected from the other side.

"Yes," shouted Mimir.

The creature yelled and whipped its hand to shake her free. Skadi pulled the sword from the monster's and fell to the ground. As soon as she landed, she made for the world troll's legs, but the beast was getting wise to her movements and jumped into the air.

"It's fast," said Mimir.

The world troll blocked out the sun, casting Skadi, Hovard, and Elfr in its shadow. Skadi noticed from the corner of her eyes that Elfr ran away from the battlefield, and Hovard launched himself into the air to put distance between him and the impending impact.

For a moment, it was as if the world troll was flying, pausing briefly high above the trees. It made a fist and roared, then began its descent back to Midgard.

Skadi widened her stance, drew strength into her legs, and launched herself with Ridill pointed forward.

"This is going to be gross," whispered Mimir.

The fist of the world troll met the tip of Skadi's sword, and Ridill tore into the creature's flesh, up through its forearm, bicep, and shoulder. She emerged on the other side, covered in blood. Skadi turned around in the sky, spun the sword, and began her descent back to Midgard after the world troll. She caught up to the creature on its way down, landed on its head, and plunged Ridill deep into its skull. She leaped off it before the troll hit the ground and sent a shockwave in every direction so powerful it lifted smaller trees out of the ground.

Skadi landed between Elfr, who was struggling to regain his footing, and the dead world troll. Hovard landed next to Elfr.

"Summon something that can fly and go back to Fensalir. I'll handle this," said Hovard.

"I have to stop her," said Elfr.

"She'll kill you," Hovard said.

"But. You better win," said Elfr.

Skadi watched their brief exchange with a straight face.

Just then, a giant eagle swept down; Elfr jumped on its back and took off as quickly as the bird had appeared.

"It's just you and me, niece," said Hovard.

"Stay focused, and you can beat him," said Mimir.

A swirl of flame formed at Hovard's feet that soon engulfed his whole body. The heat and wind it created pushed small rocks and debris across the battlefield. A tornado of fire rocketed upward into the sky.

"You took everything from me, Skadi, and for that, I will make you suffer," shouted Hovard.

Even with her enhanced ability, Skadi recognized that Hovard was fast. It didn't register right away that he was coming for her. His movements were lightning-fast. He was in her face in under a second, and his fist was in her abdomen. The force of the punch sent her flying backward into the corpse of the world troll. Where he hit her, she was burning.

She patted the flames then dodged left to avoid a second punch aimed directly at her face. Hovard blasted into the world troll, exploding its head, sending blood, brain matter, and skull fragments skyward.

Skadi leaped into the sky, and Hovard followed.

"Nowhere to go," he said.

He shot his flames in her direction.

"We're done," shouted Mimir.

Skadi spun Ridill so fast it deflected the wave of fire and rode the flame higher into the sky until Hovard let up. Above the trees and amongst the clouds, Skadi hovered until gravity regained its hold over her, and she began her fall back to Midgard. She directed her descent, so she caught the nearest tree and used Ridill to slow her fall. When she touched the ground, it was as if she had only hopped briefly into the air.

Hovard landed across from her, flames raging around him. The heat washed over Skadi and Mimir.

"You are strong, niece," said Hovard. "The Yggdrasil gifted you."

"Hovard, you can stop this whenever you want. I am not your enemy, but as long as you align yourself with the jötunn, I will fight you," said Skadi.

"For the record, I'm not aligned with the jötunn. We temporarily have the same goal. There is a difference," said Hovard.

"Whatever helps you sleep at night," said Skadi.

"I'll sleep better when you're dead," shouted Hovard.

He charged at Skadi, tearing the ground asunder. She swiped Ridill, and he ducked left and fired at her. She dropped to the ground and rolled right before leaping to her feet and swiped again. He deflected and blasted into the sky and unleashed a storm of flames down on her. She dipped, dodged, and ducked each assault, constantly on the lookout for an opportunity to counter.

The forest around them started to burn. The flames Hovard was emitting were catching onto the trees, and black smoke was rising.

Skadi saw her opportunity and charged Hovard, sword positioned for a killing blow. He fired at her, but she sliced the flame in half and emerged on the other side. Skadi cutting through the fire caught Hovard by surprise, and he jumped backward, just barely avoiding a death blow.

"You can do this," shouted Mimir.

Skadi didn't let up. She continued her pursuit, swinging Ridill violently at Hovard with hopes to catch him at least once. She had him on the defensive, but he was fast, and he was keeping his distance.

His back hit a tree. He launched into the air as Skadi swung where he'd just been and split the tree at its base. The pine fell to its side, and Hovard retreated upward.

"You will know the pain I felt," shouted Hovard. "What you did is unforgivable."

Skadi saw him lift his hands above his head, forming a fireball larger than anything he'd created before.

"You think yourself a good person, but you are a monster," he shouted before dropping the fireball in her direction.

"Skadi," shouted Mimir.

Skadi pivoted and ran from where she'd been standing. She pulled Mimir around so he wasn't on her back. The fireball hit the ground, and the explosion launched her into the air. She cradled Mimir as she crashed into the dirt.

"Thank you," said Mimir.

"Anytime," she said.

Skadi stabbed Ridill into the ground and used it for support as she pulled herself to her feet.

"He is tough," she said.

"But he is a glass sword," said Mimir. "His attacks are powerful, but his body is fragile. You just have to touch him once."

Skadi shifted Mimir back around and started walking towards Hovard, who remained hovered above. He lifted his hands overhead for a second attack, and Skadi started running.

The fireball formed again, larger this time as Skadi picked up speed. Skadi did not let Hovard out of her sight as he launched the attack. She jumped over the fireball. It hit the ground and exploded. The force of the explosion propelled her faster toward Hovard. He dodged left, but Ridill caught his side spewing blood. Skadi landed as Hovard hit the ground, his side split open.

She wiped the blood from the blade and sheathed it before turning around and walking over to her uncle. He was struggling to pick himself up off the ground, blood flowing from his mouth.

"You could have been a great uncle to Bjorn," said Skadi.

"I would never . . . not . . . for you . . . or for him," said Hovard, as he coughed up blood.

Skadi knelt in front of him as he struggled to sit up and rested on his hands.

"Either in this life or the next," said Hovard. "Revenge will be mine."

He gasped for air and fell over.

"He's gone," said Mimir.

Skadi stood up.

"Do you want to talk about it?" said Mimir.

"Where is the final root?" she said.

"Take me to the well. I will show you," said Mimir.

Skadi carried Mimir to the center of the battlefield. His eyes lit up and shined into the well. They revealed the Yggdrasil Root, and Skadi took it into her hand. She split it in half and consumed part of it.

Immediately, she felt the power of the world tree surge through her veins from the top of her head to the soles of her feet. Sparks of electricity danced around her as a white glow emanated from her body. The Midgardian soil trembled in waves, and the fires that raged were extinguished.

"As far as I know, you are now the single most powerful human to have ever lived," said Mimir.

"Then let's wrap things up back home," said Skadi.

TWENTY-SEVEN

THE SÖKKVABEKKR SWAMP SHOWDOWN

"We need to go to the Cave of the Dying," said Lofn.

"What's happened?" said Liótr.

"The jötunn killed her," said Lofn.

"Frija?" Liótr said.

"It seems so," said Lofn.

Eirdóttir stood in the middle of the crowd, surrounded by angry residents of Fensalir. Her attention had been on Dana, but it had quickly shifted in the direction of the Cave of the Dying.

"No," she whispered.

Eirdóttir fell back to the edge of the crowd. She separated, and when she was confident no one was looking, she sprouted her wings and took the sky.

Deep underground, Alver and Bjorn were growing discouraged.

"I don't think the runes are here," said Bjorn.

"I'm inclined to agree with you," Alver said.

"What now?"

"I don't see any other pathways. We can go back to the fork in the road and try that route," said Alver.

"Let's do that," Bjorn said.

Bjorn and Alver exited the cavern and began the slow, tedious trek back through the passageway from which they'd come. When they hit the fork in the road, Bjorn sensed a third presence.

"We aren't alone down here," said Bjorn.

"Is it the jötunn?" Alver said.

"Bjorn, Alver," said Eirdóttir.

"Oh, thank Odin," said Alver.

The half-human, half-Valkyrie greeted them in the passageway, and Bjorn could see the distress on her face.

"What's happened?" he said.

She shook her head.

"Frija is gone," said Eirdóttir.

"Killed?" said Bjorn.

"Yes. The jötunn got to her," said Eirdóttir.

"What do we do now?" said Alver.

"We don't have many options left," said Bjorn.

"We are three against at least four, one of which is a jötunn with immense power, and it is going to hunt us down," said Eirdóttir. "At least that is what we should expect if we don't act fast."

"What are you proposing?" said Alver.

"She thinks we should attack," said Bjorn.

"An ambush," said Eirdóttir. "Not the most honorable of approaches . . ."

"But all that is left to us in terms of options," said Alver. "I get it."

"Frija was at the Cave of the Dying, so I would assume that is where she was killed," said Bjorn.

"Safe assumption," said Eirdóttir.

"I doubt the jötunn is going to want to reveal himself to the world, so he is going to summon the council members to collect the body so they can claim they killed her," said Bjorn.

"Which means they'll probably bring her to the council hall," said Alver.

"The jötunn won't be with them; otherwise, he'll be undermining the purpose of passing her death off on them," said Eirdóttir.

"So, are we suggesting we attack the council at the council hall?" said Alver.

"Unless you two have a better plan," said Eirdóttir.

"Well, we still don't know what Dana can do. Right?" said Alver.

"That's true," said Eirdóttir.

"So, for all we know, we could be walking into an ambush and not the other way around," said Alver. "The public already thinks Frija is the bad guy. If they think the council killed her, they'll be heroes, and then the public will protect them. We need to expose them, not just attack them."

"How?" said Bjorn.

"We were just standing in it," said Alver. "The jötunn's cave. I've lived in Fensalir a long time; believe me, this is the only underground network aside from the Cave of the Dying. So, we threaten to make his location public. I doubt the jötunn will want people exploring his feeding ground and will force the council to stop us. But we tell the public where it is beforehand."

"And the council will be caught red-handed doing what it's always done," said Bjorn.

"The jötunn's bidding," said Alver.

"That could work," said Eirdóttir. "It's mildly sloppy, but it is the best plan we've got."

"Eirdóttir, I'll go with you to the council hall. Bjorn, you go to the cave. We have to act fast," said Alver.

"Going now," said Bjorn.

They all exited the cave, and Eirdóttir grabbed Alver and took off. He felt the air wash over him as she carried him through the sky, an experience he never thought he would have. She brought him back to the center of town with Alver in hand towards the council hall. She dropped him off before the public could see Eirdóttir flying, and the two walked the rest of the way. Dana was busy taking questions and did not see their approach.

Alver looked at Eirdóttir, and she nodded approvingly.

"Attention everyone," shouted Alver.

Dana was the first to look their way. She locked eyes with Eirdóttir, then Alver. The crowd followed suit.

"You have all been lied to. The posters you saw earlier that drew you here are the truth. The council is not here to protect you. They are here to protect a monster that has been killing our children. We have proof of this," shouted Alver.

"What proof?" shouted someone from within the crowd.

"A cave," shouted Alver. "A cave with the remains of our children who have been slaughtered for far too long."

There was chatter amongst the crowd.

"He is lying," shouted Dana. "This man is in cahoots with the witch and is trying to distract you all from the truth."

"Come with us," Alver shouted. "If I'm lying, you'll know soon enough."

Dana and Alver locked eyes.

"What is there to lose?" shouted someone from within the crowd. "He lost his son too. Might as well hear him out."

Bjorn scurried across Fensalir as fast as his feet would take him, and not before long, he had eyes on the Cave of the Dying. He spied Liótr and Lofn landing by the entrance. He watched them enter then moved closer, paying close attention to his surroundings, so no one discovered him prematurely.

Bjorn's heart was thumping in his chest. This journey would soon end, and he honestly had no clue how. He hoped for the best but knew the odds.

He inched closer and closer to the entrance of the cave. As he got near, he could hear talking.

Lofn and Liótr stood opposite the Jötunn. Between them and the monster was the body of Frija.

"You two need to diffuse the situation at the council hall," said the jötunn. "Take her body and show the people that she is dead. Tell them you killed her."

"We're on it," said Liótr.

"Don't delay," said the jötunn, before disappearing.

"He really killed her," said Lofn leaning over Frija's body and inspecting her.

"She had no power left," said Liótr. "Whether she was what we thought or not, in the end, it didn't matter."

Liótr picked up Frija's body and tossed her over his shoulder.

"What's our narrative?" said Lofn.

"What do you mean?" said Liótr.

"I mean, people are going to want to know how this went down. We didn't kill her," said Lofn.

"She attacked us, and we stopped her," said Liótr.

"She attacked us?" said Lofn. "She was on the run. I think we need to do a little better than that."

"Then you come up with something. You're the death whisperer. Just use one of their stories," said Liótr.

Bjorn peeked his head inside the cave and saw Liótr and Lofn arguing. He didn't see the jötunn and withdrew.

"If Alver and Eirdóttir managed to get the crowd's attention, they would have done it by now," whispered Bjorn. "Now's the time."

Bjorn jumped in front of the cave's entrance.

"Hey, you idiots," he shouted. "We found your little secret, and we're going to let all of Fensalir know. You think you have a problem now? Just wait until the jötunn's hideout is discovered."

"There's that brat. Skadi's kid," said Liótr to Lofn. "Did he just say they found the cave?"

Lofn nodded.

"The jötunn is going to have a problem with that," said Liótr.

Bjorn ran off. Liótr started after him, but Lofn grabbed his arm.

"What?" said Liótr.

"This is a trap," said Lofn. "Why would he tell us they plan on exposing the jötunn's cave?"

"Even if it is a trap, if they expose it, that's still a problem for us," said Liótr.

"Is it?" said Lofn. "Remember what I said. This does not end well for any of us."

"Do you want to go down like Petronilla?" said Liótr.

"I'm not going," said Lofn.

"It's your funeral," said Liótr.

"No. It's yours," said Lofn.

The two looked at one another then parted ways. Liótr carried Frija's corpse out of the cave in pursuit of Bjorn.

"Dumbass is going to get himself killed," whispered Lofn.

Bjorn waited for a moment for the two council members to exit the cave.

"Come on, you fools, follow me," he whispered.

No one showed immediately, and he debated taunting them a second time. Just then, though, he spied Liótr leave the cave and start following him.

"Get back here, you little bastard," shouted Liótr.

Bjorn pivoted and started running full speed.

"Be ready," whispered Bjorn.

Alver and Eirdóttir led a crowd of folks from the council hall towards Sökkvabekkr Swamp. With them was Dana Robert, who had no choice but to tag along. Alver would often look back to make sure Dana was not doing anything that would harm them and that the crowd was still with them even though the crowd was causing a raucous.

"Is this going to work?" said Eirdóttir.

"I hope," said Alver.

They reached the wooden structure through which Bjorn and Alver had accessed the cave earlier. There, they stopped the crowd.

"This is where we have to send people down one at a time. This shed leads underground," said Alver.

"Underground?" shouted someone in the crowd. "One at a time. You never said anything about going underground."

"It's a cave," said Eirdóttir. "The jötunn that has been killing your children and feeds on them in a cave."

"I'm not going down there," shouted another person from the crowd. "If that is a jötunn's feeding ground, you're not going to catch me walking right into it."

"They have a point," said Eirdóttir.

"Fine. I will go down and bring you back proof, then I will insist you see it for yourself," said Alver.

"Wait," whispered Eirdóttir. "I'll go."

"No," said Alver. "If you go, Dana could easily overpower me, and we'd lose any ground we've made, but if I go and the jötunn is down there, at least we'll still have you and Bjorn. I have to do this."

Eirdóttir didn't reply right away, and then after a few seconds, she nodded.

"Good luck," she said.

"Thanks," he whispered.

Alver moved to open the door.

"I will bring back a skull," he said. "Proof."

He descended the well, and when he hit bottom, he lit up his torch. The cold was just as abrasive as it was the first time, even more so it seemed. He pulled his pelt tighter to his body.

"Please don't be down here," he said to himself.

Alver started walking down the dark passageway, lit up poorly by the torch. He moved cautiously but with purpose. Soon he was at the fork in the road and went left just like before.

Above ground, there was grumbling in the crowd. Eirdóttir stood by the door of the wooden structure and kept an eye on Dana. Dana kept her distance but was watching Eirdóttir like a wolf watches its prey. There was an energy brewing, and it would soon explode. Someone just had to light the fuse.

Alver crept through the passageway, extremely cognizant of his surroundings. His heart had never beat faster. He was sweating through his pelt despite the cold, and his grip on the torch was slipping due to his clammy palms.

He stopped to wipe his forehead.

"Relax, Alver," he whispered to himself. "Relax."

He continued. Every step was heavy. He had to force himself to move. Dread was starting to take him.

"Remember who you are doing this for. For Buna. For Dofri," he whispered.

Soon enough, he arrived at the cavern. Nothing had changed, but he could sense something was wrong.

"Am I going crazy?" he whispered to himself.

Alver stepped out of the passage and into the cavern. He made an immediate move for the pile of skeletons. There was no desire to linger.

Dana moved towards Eirdóttir.

"What is this?" she said. "What are you two doing? You know this is a farce."

"Why are you so on edge?" said Eirdóttir.

"This is bullshit, and you know it," whispered Dana. "The jötunn will rip you apart and eat you. That's if I don't kill you first."

"Keep up your threats," said Eirdóttir. "You don't scare me."

"Oh yea?" said Dana grabbing Eirdóttir by the arm.

She quickly let go, but Eirdóttir got the message. Her arm was frostbitten.

"So that's your power," she whispered.

Alver picked up one of the skulls and turned to return to the surface. As he made his way across the cavern, his gut sank when he heard footsteps behind him.

"I would put that down," said a voice emanating from the darkness.

Alver felt like his heart was going to burst out of his chest. He turned around and standing over him was the jötunn. His black eyes flickered in the light of the torch.

"To be honest, you had me a worried when you ran off, but with Frija gone, my concerns lessened," said the jötunn.

Alver slowly took a step backward.

"You people have become quite the thorn," the jötunn said.

Alver continued to back away.

"But like any thorn, you only have to pluck it out, and the problem is solved," said the jötunn.

Alver stepped away, increasing the gap between him and the creature, but then the jötunn sprang on him. He grabbed Alver by the waist and pulled him in tightly. Alver dropped the skull and struggled to get free. The jötunn tightened his grip.

"Let. Me. Go," Alver struggled to say.

The crowd above ground was growing anxious. There was a consensus forming that they had waited for answers for long enough. First at the council hall and now at the tunnel underground. Eirdóttir could sense the anxiety.

"Where is Alver?" she said to herself before grabbing the door.

"Where are you going?" said someone within the crowd.

"I will be just a moment," she said.

Eirdóttir opened the door and shut it upon entering.

"I know he said he should be the only one to go, but . . ." she said.

She dropped to the ground, not bothering the climb. Unlike Alver and Bjorn, being half Valkyrie granted her gifts that even the enhanced Bjorn did not have, and one of those gifts was the ability to perceive light in the darkest of areas. Under normal circumstances, this ability was meant for ushering those to Hel, where light did not exist.

Eirdóttir charged down the passageway to the fork in the road. She stopped and listened to determine which way to go.

Alver felt his bones wanting to fracture as the jötunn squeezed tighter.

"Go. To. Hel," Alver managed to get out.

"You first," said the jötunn.

This was it. Alver prepared for death. He closed his eyes, and Dofri and Buna flashed before them. Then there was a loud crunch. He had convinced himself he was done for, but when he opened his eyes, he saw Eirdóttir pushing the jötunn across the cavern. The crunch had been the skull; he'd fallen on it when Eirdóttir saved him.

"Can you stand?" she shouted, noticing his subtle movement.

"I think so," said Alver pulling himself to his feet.

He struggled, but he managed to get to two legs.

"Go," she shouted.

Alver looked down. The skull was in fragments. He looked left and saw another pile of skeletons. Alver hobbled over and grabbed the nearest skull he could find.

"What are you doing?" shouted Eirdóttir. "Get out of here."

"I'm going," he said.

He sprang to his feet and ran out of the cavern.

The jötunn was strong, and despite her surprise attack, it was not phased in the slightest bit. But the creature had dropped Alver to catch the half-Valkyrie, and her momentum had pushed the beast backward. She flapped her massive wings to aid her, but the jötunn quickly took control of the situation, digging his feet into the cave floor and stopping her flight path.

"You should not have come here," said the jötunn to Eirdóttir.

The creature grabbed her forearms and lifted her into the air, up and over his head. Then he fell backward, bringing her down hard on the ground. The jötunn knew he had knocked the air out of her, but, she bounced back quickly and was once again in pursuit of him. He, however, had shifted his attention towards Alver. Because his attention had diverted, she managed to tackle him into the wall to the left of the passageway, just barely saving Alver.

The jötunn tossed Eirdóttir against the wall of the cavern. The force with which she hit the wall knocked her unconscious, and she collapsed on the ground. He then turned its attention towards the passageway through which Alver had escaped.

Dana watched Eirdóttir disappear inside the building. She then looked at the crowd of folks who had followed Alver and Eirdóttir to the edge of Sökkvabekkr Swamp and could tell that confusion had overtaken the majority of those there.

"You see," said Dana. "This is all a farce. These two dragged you all out here for nothing but a charade. They want to distract you from the truth. Whatever they dig up from underground, if they dig up anything at all, it will be nothing but a lie. My colleagues and I have always had the people of Fensalir's best interest at heart. These two are scrambling to deceive you."

"She has a point," shouted someone from within the crowd. "What are we doing here?"

"Let's give them more time. I want to see what proof they have," said another person.

"We are wasting valuable time; we could be searching for the witch," said a third person.

"Valuable time indeed," said Dana. "Every moment we spend here, the witch Frija is out there plotting, getting one over on us all."

Alver could hear the skirmish between Eirdóttir and the jötunn growing fainter and fainter as he ran through the dark passageway. He had the skull in hand and was hoping Bjorn's timing would be impeccable because if he arrived up top without Bjorn's strength to support him, Dana would surely make short work of him, no matter what power she had.

He hit the fork and picked up speed. He was almost at the ladder. Then he felt the trembling of the ground beneath his feet. The floor and walls were crumbling. He grabbed the ladder and started the ascent.

Alver struggled to make the climb due to his injuries received during his brief encounter with the jötunn and because in his right hand was the skull of a child, but he managed as best he could towards the surface. Rung after rung, he gained ground. But barreling down the passageway was the jötunn, and it was hot on Alver's trail.

He was nearing the top of the ladder. He could see the streaks of light from the shed and dust motes floating in them. But the trembling he felt in the passageway was making its way up to the ladder as well. The walls were shaking, and dirt was kicking up into the air.

He looked down, and his eyes went wide.

"Shit," he said.

The jötunn was barreling up the ladder, baring its teeth. Alver quickened his pace, but he honestly couldn't move much faster, handicapped by the skull and his injuries. At this rate, he would the monster would catch him in seconds.

He looked up, leaned back, and threw the skull the final few rungs. It landed in the dirt at the bottom of the door.

"Go to Hel," he shouted down at the jötunn, preparing for the inevitable.

Eirdóttir got up on all fours and shook her head. Her ears were ringing. She couldn't remember anything ever hitting her that hard. Despite her ability to see clearly in the dark, her vision was blurry.

"How strong is that thing?" she said to herself.

Eirdóttir hurried after the jötunn to intercept it before it got to Alver. Because the passageway confined her wingspan, making it so she could not fly, she ran as fast as possible.

The jötunn reached out to grab Alver, but Eirdóttir caught him. Alver saw this and, with both his hands free, used the opportunity to clear the ladder.

He looked over the ledge and saw Eirdóttir and the jötunn tussling violently in the confined space, but the imbalance in power was overwhelmingly in favor of the beast, and the creature sent her tumbling.

Alver grabbed the skull he'd tossed ahead of him.

He opened the door and said, "Here it is. Here is the proof you need."

But there was no one there. The crowd had disappeared.

"Where did everyone go?" shouted Alver.

"People will trust whoever provides the greatest comfort. You misplaced your faith," said Dana.

"What did you do?" said Alver.

"Nothing at all. They decided they were tired of waiting," said Dana. "Your narrative proved too unsettling. People would rather have an enemy they can see and know exist even if it's the wrong one."

Alver looked at the skull in his hand.

"If only they had been able to see this," he whispered.

"It was probably pretty cold down there, am I right?" said Dana. "That's because the jötunn is a frost giant from Jotunheim. I always thought that I had jotnar blood in my lineage, so when my powers mani-fested, I was not surprised at all at what I could do."

A feverishly cold wind emanated from Dana. Ice formed at her feet and spread across the ground in all directions.

Alver scurried backward.

"No, no, no, no," he said.

The ice nearly reached him, but then his feet left the ground. He looked up and saw Bjorn had him by the collar of his pelt. The two landed many feet away.

"Get to safety," Bjorn said.

Alver nodded and ran off.

Bjorn saw that Lióti, who had been pursuing Bjorn, per the plan, touched ground alongside his council colleague Dana. At the same time, the shed atop the underground passageway exploded, and the jötunn emerged in all its dark glory.

The three stared down Bjorn, who stood alone. Sökkvabekkr Swamp was to his right and their left. Himinbjorg Mountain loomed over them all. Lióti dropped Frija's body.

"Give up, boy," said the jötunn.

Bjorn took his bow from his back and armed it with an arrow. Up from the remains of the shed emerged Eirdóttir. She touched down next to Bjorn. A breeze crossed the ground between them and their foes.

"I'm glad you're okay. But I'm afraid this will be the death of us," Eirdóttir whispered to Bjorn. "The jötunn is too powerful."

"We can't die. Too many people are counting on us," he whispered back.

Bjorn noticed Eirdóttir glanced at him from the corner of her eyes and gave a slight nod.

"Kill them," said the jötunn.

The two councilmen started moving towards Bjorn and Eirdóttir as Bjorn and Eirdóttir approached the councilmen. The wind intensified.

Bjorn beat his chest and let out a guttural yell before charging full speed. Lióti and Dana did the same.

"I'll take the Valkyrie," said Lióti.

"That leaves you to me," said Dana to Bjorn.

Alver stopped to catch his breath and looked back to see the clash beginning. He watched as forces collided that shook Fensalir.

"I have to do something," he said between gasps for air. "But what?"

He spied the skull in his hand and ran back towards the center of town.

"If they can only see the truth," he said to himself.

Liótr tackled Eirdóttir to the ground. She tussled with him in the dirt and managed to get the upper hand. She pinned him down, pulled back her fist, and aimed to knock him unconscious, but he scrambled to freedom, knocking her off him.

While she struggled with her combatant, Eirdóttir could see Bjorn having trouble with Dana. The council leader was impossible for him to get close to since she would freeze every arrow before it got within twenty feet of her. Eirdóttir could also see that Bjorn's quiver was running low. He was about to pull back another when she noticed he stopped. "What are you doing?" she said.

"Eirdóttir," said Bjorn. "It gets cold in Hel, does it not?"

"It does," Eirdóttir shouted.

"Could a Valkyrie survive there?" said Bjorn.

"Oh no, you don't," shouted Dana.

Dana powered up a blast of ice and launched it at Bjorn. Eirdóttir made sure he cleared the attack and was okay before going after Dana.

Dana pursued Bjorn, but Eirdóttir flapped her mighty wings and launched after her. She grabbed Dana by the hair, snapping her backward, and slammed her to the ground, knocking her unconscious. Upon defeating Dana, she saw Bjorn's knee connect with Liótr's face. The two council members were out.

"We did it," said Eirdóttir.

"Fight's not over yet," said Bjorn.

Eirdóttir turned to face the jötunn, but a cawing caught her's and Bjorn's attention. She looked up and saw a giant bird swooping onto the battlefield and on its back, Elfr. Then from the tree line, a pack of wolves quickly accompanied by bears and trolls.

"Couldn't be done without me," shouted Elfr.

His mind-controlled creatures of the forest surrounded Eirdóttir and Bjorn. They stood with their backs to one another. Then, one of the trolls stepped forth to grab Dana and Liótr. Eirdóttir saw Bjorn snap the beast's wrists, and it retreated.

"What do we do?" said Eirdóttir.

"We don't let them wake these two up. That's for sure," he said.

Elfr brought his bird just overhead and unsheathed Dáinsleif. Eirdóttir observed the jötunn see the weapon and crack a small smile.

"Kill them," said Elfr.

All the creatures started in on Eirdóttir and Bjorn at once. It became a free-for-all.

The citizens of Fensalir could hear the howls and yelps of wolves meeting fists while trying to tear flesh far from the battlefield.

Alver stopped running again to catch his breath and look back.

"What's going on now?" he said.

He shook his head.

"Gotta keep going," he said.

Alver made his way into town and saw the crowd from earlier splitting up.

"Hey," he shouted.

A few stopped and looked at him, but not everyone.

"Hey, you guys," shouted Alver.

Now, the remainder of the crowd stopped and turned in his direction.

"What is it?" said the person nearest him.

Alver held up the skull.

A man walked up and took the skull into his hand. He inspected it.

"You got this underground?" said the man.

"I told you before. The jötunn has been feeding on our children in a cave deep under the town."

"What's he got there?" said someone further back in the crowd.

The man held up the skull so everyone could see.

The creatures that Elfr commanded were proving to be a lot. They were swarming Bjorn and Eirdóttir, and despite the duo's strength, there were two of them and what seemed like an unending horde of ferocious animals.

"I'm not sure . . ." said Eirdóttir. "How much longer I can keep this up."

Bjorn grabbed a wolf and threw it into one of the trolls. It knocked the giant beast on its butt. A bear grabbed Liótr by the arm and started to drag him away, but Bjorn saw that Eirdóttir intercepted, severely injuring the bear's paw, then kicked the creature square in its chest. The animal ran off.

"Grab her," said Bjorn, pointing at Dana.

As Eirdóttir did as he instructed, Bjorn grabbed hold of Liótr.

"Oh no, you don't," said Elfr.

He swooped in on the back of his bird and swiped at Bjorn with Dáinsleif. He moved to deflect it with a dagger he kept on his person.

"Dodge, don't block," shouted Eirdóttir.

At the last minute, he did as she instructed.

"Not that weapon," shouted Eirdóttir. "It's guaranteed death for whoever it cuts. Even the slightest wound caused by it will never heal. You would bleed out forever."

Elfr brought his bird back around just as a massive troll came for Dana. Eirdóttir batted the troll away but not before it got a hold on Dana and pulled her with it. Elfr and the bird drew Bjorn's attention, and while he was momentarily distracted, a wolf managed to pull Liótr away.

"No," Bjorn shouted.

The creatures lined Dana and Liótr up, and Elfr got off his bird next to them.

"Wake up, you idiots," he said before mentally kickstarting their minds then actually kicking them each in the side.

They stirred.

"Where is Lofn?" said Elfr.

"She . . . chose not to fight," said Liótr, his wits slowly coming back to him.

"You two let yourselves get knocked around by these two brats. What is wrong with you?" said Elfr.

"They're strong," said Liótr.

"And you aren't?" said Elfr.

"Is the woman dead?" said Dana.

"Skadi?" said Elfr. "I don't know."

"What do you mean you don't know?" said Dana.

"I mean, Hovard said he'd handle it," said Elfr.

"And you let him?" said Dana.

"You weren't there. The circumstances were tricky," said Elfr.

"I hope you knew what you were doing for your sake," said Dana.

"I saved you fools," said Elfr.

"Dana's right. Skadi better be dead, or you're going to have a problem on your hands," said Liótr.

Elfr looked past his two colleagues at the jötunn who was standing by the water's edge.

"He's been letting you guys fight and not helping?" said Elfr.

"Why bother giving us these powers if we aren't supposed to use them on his behalf?" said Dana.

"Yeah, but I thought that was under normal circumstances. This seems a bit different," said Elfr.

"We are peasants to him," said Dana. "Expendable. Don't forget that."

"Duly noted," said Elfr.

Elfr extended a hand and helped Dana to her feet. She did the same for Liótr.

"What now?" said Elfr.

"We kill these two, and then we go make sure Hovard finished the job with Skadi. After that, we find our friend Lofn and destroy her for turning her back on us," said Dana.

"She is a coward," said Liótr.

"Let's make short work of them," said Elfr.

"With pleasure," said Liótr.

Alver led the crowd of concerned citizens back through the forest towards the edge of Sökkvabekkr Swamp. Everyone could hear the raging battle, which piqued their interest beyond the discovery of the skull.

Alver instructed the crowd to stop as they approached the edge of the battlefield. Through the line of trees, they could see Eirdóttir and Bjorn struggling against a horde of various creatures and the three council members. Then, he turned back to the crowd.

"This is what I wanted to show you," said Alver. "Look over to the left. You see that creature by the water?"

"Yes," said one person.

"That is the jötunn. He is the mastermind behind everything that's happened here, and he is what has been killing our kids. The jötunn corrupted the council members of our town by offering them special gifts, and they've been protecting him ever since," said Alver.

"Who are the council members fighting?" said another person.

"The boy is Bjorn. He and his mother were tasked to destroy the jötunn by Frija, who the council members wanted you to believe was the enemy. His mother is still out in Midgard. We don't know if she is alive. The girl is a half-Valkyrie. Her mother was a friend of Frija but was killed aiding Skadi. Those two are right now the only ones that stand between your kids and that monster," said Alver.

"We've been deceived," said a person in the crowd. "How could this have happened?"

"It's okay," said Alver. "What matters is what you do now."

"What can we do?" said the same person.

There was a loud bang as Liótr slammed Bjorn across the battlefield.

"These guys are fighting at a level beyond us," said a person in the crowd.

"And our people are losing," said Alver.

"There is strength in numbers," someone said. "They can't kill us all."

"They're strong," said Alver. "But we are stronger."

"My daughter would still be here if it weren't for that monster," said a woman who stepped up to the front of the crowd. "I couldn't even have a burial because there was no body. I'll fight."

"My son was found mutilated," said a man. "I'll fight too."

"Jón would be twelve now if he hadn't been killed two years ago," said another woman. "Count me in."

Slowly, one by one, all the crowd rallied.

Bjorn slammed a troll to the ground then jumped to avoid Dana's blast of ice. The troll caught the attack shattering it into one hundred pieces. Bjorn fired an arrow at Elfr, but one of his creatures leaped to protect him and took the arrow in its side. Bjorn pivoted and charged after Liótr. He swiped at him, but he dropped to the ground, and Bjorn flew over the top. He landed and quickly went for another attack, but before he could strike, a wolf bit his wrist, providing Liótr with a chance to get away.

"We're being overwhelmed," said Bjorn. "We need to focus on the one with the sword."

"Not a chance," said Dana.

She rained cold waves of ice over Bjorn and Eirdóttir. The pair scattered.

Bjorn and Liótr exchanged blows. Each hit was seismic and made the ground beneath them tremble. Their physicality was immense, and they both fought like experts. Liótr was larger than Bjorn, but it made no difference.

And he could see that despite Eirdóttir's Valkyrie physiology which made her a better match for Dana's elemental control over ice, she was not fairing much better than he was. Dana's powers were still very much impactful, though not entirely lethal. However, Eirdóttir was struggling to get in close and deal Dana some damage.

But while both Bjorn and Eirdóttir could compete with Liótr and Dana, every time they did get close enough to finishing either combatant, one of Elfr's creatures would be there to stop them, and then Elfr would lurk with Dáinsleif, creating an ever-present, inevitable doom. And watching it all was the jötunn.

"This is impossible," said Eirdóttir with her back to Bjorn's. "We're making no ground against the grunts."

"I brought help," shouted Alver.

Standing at the edge of the forest was Alver and lining up on both sides of him were hundreds of people from the town of Fensalir.

Bjorn saw Liótr, Elfr, and Dana look towards the wall of humans in disbelief. Then he quickly noticed, Elfr's creatures turn their attention away from him and Eirdóttir and start charging the tree line. But as they did, each of the townsfolk unsheathed a sword or held up an ax they'd brought from home.

"For Fensalir," shouted Alver. "For our children."

"Yes," shouted Bjorn.

The people of Fensalir started running at the Elfr's creatures and greeted teeth and paws with swords and axes. The clash was of an epic scale.

Bjorn turned his attention back to Dana, Elfr, and Liótr. The three council members took a step back.

"Enough," said the jötunn.

The dark beast descended on the battlefield between Bjorn and Eirdóttir and the council members.

"I'll do it myself," he said.

Bjorn's legs started shaking. Then he felt Eirdóttir put her hand on his shoulder.

"We can do this," she said.

"I know," said Bjorn.

"You two will make for quite the meal," said the jötunn. "Once I've killed you, I will consume you. The power that you've contracted from the World Tree will be exquisite. And you, Valkyrie. Your kind has always been out of my reach, so I'm excited to see what you taste like. You see—"

The jötunn was cut short. Bjorn barely saw it happen—Eirdóttir struck with her sword, but it snapped upon impact, and all that remained was the hilt and a look of disbelief on her face.

The jötunn laughed.

"You think you can stop me. Look around you at all this chaos. It's only going to get worse as Fimbulwinter begins. You think you humans are unified? You just have a common enemy. When the scarcity begins, you'll turn on each other," said the jötunn. "I would say you'll see, but you two won't live long enough to experience that nightmare. Maybe I am merciful."

"You're wrong," said Bjorn. "Humans look out for each other."

"Is that so? Then why does your Great Uncle Hovard have such a vendetta against your mother? It's a shame you won't get to ask her. I would very much enjoy seeing the look on your face if she told you the truth," said the jötunn.

Bjorn formed fists and dug into the palms of his hands so hard that blood seeped through his fingers.

"Easy, Bjorn. He is just trying to rile you up," said Eirdóttir.

"The table has been set," said the jötunn. "Now, let us begin."

The ground started to pulsate outwardly from the jötunn's position and grew increasingly violent as dark clouds formed overhead. Lightning strikes touched down all over the battlefield and the swamp. Elfr, Liótr, and Dana quickly retreated.

"This is going to be tougher than we thought," said Bjorn.

"You are fools," said the jötunn. "I was preparing for Ragnarök. I have more than enough power to crush you two."

TWENTY-EIGHT

HOPE

Bjorn took Eirdóttir's extended hand and got up on his feet. His face, like hers, was bloodied and bruised. She was without a sword, and his quiver was empty.

"He is toying with us," said Bjorn.

"I'm aware," said Eirdóttir.

"He seems to have no weakness and boundless stamina. I've never seen anything like him," said Bjorn.

"If we don't figure out a way to hurt him, this town is doomed," said Eirdóttir looking around the clearing.

Scattered about the battlefield were human bodies and dead creatures. A handful of resilient warriors and Alver were still attempting to clash with Dana, Liótr, and Elfr, but the three enhanced council members were quickly overpowering them. The lesser skilled fighters had scattered. Morale was depleted.

The jötunn descended from the sky and landed before Bjorn and Eirdóttir.

"How are you so strong?" said Bjorn. "The jotnar are just giants. They're not gods."

The jötunn laughed.

"The jotnar are not just giants from Jotunheim, though . . . to be fair, that is where I am from. No. The jotnar exists everywhere. The hammer-wielding protector of Asgard is part jötunn. His mother Jörð is a jötunn. His grandmother on his father's side, Bestla, was part jötunn as well, which makes Odin himself part jötunn. In fact, the primeval being born from the venom that dripped from the icy rivers of Élivágar and lived in the void Ginnungagap and from which the nine realms were created, Ymir, is the original jötunn. The being that your people worship and whom your mother is named after is a jötunn. So, you see, we are a proud and diverse race of beings, superior in every way possible to all creatures of the nine realms, especially humans," said the jötunn.

"Thanks for explaining your family tree," said Eirdóttir.

"So, who are you in all of this?" said Bjorn.

The jötunn smiled.

"That's not important," he said.

The jötunn blasted forward and hit Bjorn. Bjorn blocked the assault, but the impact sent him flying into the air. As Bjorn struggled to get his bearings, he noticed, the jötunn turn his attention to Eirdóttir and did the same to her. However, she could use her wings to steady herself, and moments later, Bjorn realized he was resting in her arms. But as soon as they touched the ground, the jötunn was on top of them again.

Bjorn quickly realized the jötunn was going for Eirdóttir first and tried to intervene, but he was too slow, and the jötunn grabbed her by the head and slammed her face into the dirt. Bjorn jumped on the jötunn's back, but the creature pulled him free and chucked him into the swamp. The last thing he saw before dipping beneath the surface of the water was the jötunn stepping on Eirdóttir and digging his foot into her back, preventing her from getting up.

"I've had enough of you," said the jötunn. "I've known quite a few Valkyries in my day, and none have been so problematic."

The jötunn leaned over and grabbed Eirdóttir's wings and, with one quick, powerful yank, ripped them from her body. She howled as blood spewed from her back. The jötunn laughed and tossed the wings aside. The beast kicked her, so she rolled over. He knelt by her side and put his hand around her throat.

"I'm going to carve you two up," said the jötunn. "Normally, it's quick and painless for these kids. I kill them before consuming them. I am not entirely heartless. But you and him . . . Skadi's boy . . . you two I'm going to torture."

"You're . . . just . . . a . . . coward," said Eirdóttir.

"I am a survivor," said the jötunn. "And you two are in my way."

He pulled back one of his clawed hands and aimed for her eyes.

"At least this way, you won't see what I do to you," said the jötunn with a smile.

But before he could strike, he was gone.

Bjorn slammed his entire weight into the jötunn and knocked the creature free of Eirdóttir. He quickly turned and helped her to her feet.

"You're done," said Bjorn. "Get out of here."

"And go where?" she said.

He spied the jötunn getting to his feet.

"Is there any way to stop this thing?" said Bjorn rhetorically.

"My wings," said Eirdóttir, touching her back where they once were.

"Will you heal? Can they grow back?" said Bjorn.

"It's like losing a limb," she said.

The jötunn was now back on his feet. Bjorn and the creature made eye contact.

"We tried," said Bjorn.

The ground shook as the beast shot across the battlefield, his right arm outstretched. Bjorn and Eirdóttir each braced for their demise, and just as it was about to come, someone knocked them from the monster's path. Standing where they had just been was Alver, impaled on the jötunn's arm.

"Alver," shouted Bjorn.

"Dofri . . ." he said, coughing up blood. "I'll see you . . . soon. You two . . . beat this . . . thing."

The jötunn withdrew his hand, and Alver fell to the ground.

"Hmph," said the jötunn. "He gave you only a mere second extra to live."

The creature turned his attention to Bjorn and Eirdóttir, who were composing themselves. But before he could deal them a death blow, a look of alarm overtook the jötunn's face. Bjorn saw him turn his attention away from them and towards the tree line just like when the townsfolk had arrived, but with far more concern.

"What's coming?" whispered Bjorn.

A boom rang out across all Fensalir, and the trees of the forest shook. The ground quaked, and then it was over.

From the edge of the forest emerged Skadi, wielding Ridill with Mimir hanging from the belt of her pelt. She walked across the battlefield towards Bjorn, Eirdóttir, and the jötunn.

"Nice of you to join us," said the jötunn.

"Mom," whispered Bjorn. "She made it."

"You're just in time. I was about to end the life of your son and his little friend," said the jötunn.

Skadi continued walking.

"Not going to say goodbye?" said the jötunn.

Skadi looked the jötunn's way but did not say a word.

"Fine," shouted the jötunn.

The monster raised his arm in the air and, with extreme quickness, brought it down where Bjorn was standing but hit nothing but air. Skadi could see his confusion when he looked her way and saw that Bjorn and Eirdóttir were safely by her side, many feet away.

"That's impossible," the creature said.

Skadi stood with Bjorn and Eirdóttir.

"You fought well," said Skadi. "Here."

She held out the other half of the Yggdrasil root.

"Split it. It'll heal both of your injuries," said Skadi. "I'll take over from here."

"Mom, he is too much. Let us help you."

"You've done enough," she said and embraced her boy. "I want you to take Mimir with you."

She handed Bjorn the head.

"Who is this?"

"The name is Mimir. Wisest man alive," said Mimir.

"You're a head," said Bjorn.

"I'm quite aware," said Mimir.

"Where did you come from?" said Bjorn.

"That's a long story," Mimir said.

"And one we don't have time for," said Skadi.

"Mom, watch out," shouted Bjorn.

Dana launched a wave of ice at Skadi, but she cut through the blast with Ridill, slicing up to Dana. She put one fist in the woman's abdomen. Dana grabbed her stomach, fell to her knees, and passed out.

"How dare you," shouted Liótr as he charged Skadi.

In the blink of an eye, she slipped out of sight and reappeared behind him. She hit him on the back of his head, knocking him unconscious. He fell to his knees then his face hit the dirt.

"Oh shit," whispered Elfr.

Skadi turned her sights on him, but the jötunn slid up next to him as she did so.

"Give me the sword," said the jötunn.

Skadi watched Elfr hand the creature the weapon, then raise his hands and back away.

"Skadi, this is it for you," said the jötunn.

She acknowledged the creature with a glance.

"Your time is up," she said.

"My time is up?" laughed the jötunn. "Oh, I'm going to enjoy this."

"Not as much as I will," said Skadi.

The remaining residents of Fensalir, who had come to fight, fled the battlefield. Three of which carried Alver's remains with them.

"You got this, mom," said Bjorn.

Skadi nodded. Then Bjorn and Eirdóttir fled also, stopping just to grab the body of Frija. The ground trembled as arcs of electricity danced between Skadi and the jötunn. The clouds that had formed darkened, and a violent wind whipped up across the land.

"If she fails . . ." said Eirdóttir.

"She won't," said Bjorn.

"But if she does, it'll be a bloodbath unlike anything Midgard has ever seen," Eirdóttir said.

"We should make sure that beast doesn't have any more allies. Let's find Elfr and Lofn," said Mimir.

"What are you head?" said Bjorn.

"An advisor. I helped your mom find that sword she's using. It'll defend against Dáinsleif," said Mimir.

"But will it help her win?" said Bjorn.

"I can't tell you for a fact that she has the strength or skill to defeat this monster, but I do know she has the motivation and will and, in my experience, will has proven the deciding factor in more battles than not," said Mimir. "That said, she may still need help."

Ridill met Dáinsleif in an epic clash of powerful dwarven swords. Lightning-fast strikes were thwarted and countered by the jötunn and Skadi. Each blow could easily cut down lesser beings, but the two were far more than that.

Skadi pivoted to catch the jötunn off guard, but the creature was just as fast and blocked, then ducked, then countered. She parried his attack, and the two danced with colorful swordplay.

"It's going to take a lot more than a magic sword and a power boost from the World Tree to give you an edge on me. I survived the Great War, and I will survive you," said the jötunn.

The jötunn brought the sword down, and Skadi dodged left. The weapon missed her and split the ground, forming a trench big enough to swallow a person in their entirety. She countered, but the jötunn deflected.

Bjorn, carrying Mimir and with Eirdóttir following, ran into the town proper searching for Elfr.

"They have to be around here somewhere," said Eirdóttir.

"Not Lofn. She didn't show up to fight," said Bjorn.

"I can tell you exactly where they are if you give me time," said Mimir.

"How?" said Bjorn.

"One moment," said Mimir, and he closed his eyes.

Bjorn observed his rapid eye movement under his eyelids.

"I got Elfr, but I can't see Lofn," said Mimir.

"How?" said Eirdóttir.

"I can see through the eyes of Odin's ravens Hugin and Munin, and they are watching this part of Midgard. But that's not important. What's concerning is that I can't find Lofn," said Mimir. "Which means she's may not be in Midgard."

"Is that an immediate concern?" said Bjorn.

"No," said Mimir.

"Then where is Elfr?" said Eirdóttir.

"Not far," Mimir said.

Skadi struck at the jötunn, and the creature blocked. However, the jötunn returned the attack, and Skadi countered.

"I can't believe this, but it seems we are too evenly matched," said the jötunn.

Skadi attacked again, but the jötunn blocked again.

"The World Tree was supposed . . ." said Skadi.

"To give you an edge over me?" said the jötunn. "It must be so disheartening to have worked so hard for something and to still fall short."

Skadi ignored his taunts and launched into an awesome barrage of sword strikes, but the jötunn defended each one perfectly.

"Face it," said the jötunn. He countered the final strike. And he hit her so hard she went flying. "I am still your superior."

Skadi hit the ground and tumbled to a stop. She got up and wiped the blood and sweat from her brow. The jötunn followed up his attack with another quick assault to which Skadi deflected every blow, but she was pushed back towards the edge of the swamp.

"Just one good hit from this sword, and you're done," said the jötunn.

"Fully aware," said Skadi.

The jötunn inched towards her, and Skadi stepped back. Her foot fell in the water of Sökkvabekkr Swamp, and she quickly pulled it free.

"You're done," said the jötunn.

The jötunn leaped at her, but Skadi fell backward, and as the monster flew over the top of her, she stabbed Ridill upward and pierced the creature through his midsection. The beast howled and crashed into the water. Skadi scrambled to her feet and repositioned herself on dry land.

An explosion of water rocketed into the air as the jötunn emerged from the swamp. The water rained down on Skadi, and a lightning strike touched the ground behind her.

The wound the sword had caused healed before Skadi's eyes.

"Do better," said the jötunn.

Eirdóttir, Bjorn, and Mimir kicked in the door of a cabin in town, and a giant wolf greeted them. Bjorn made quick work of the animal.

"Wait," shouted Elfr, who was hiding in the corner.

"Give it up," said Bjorn. "You're done."

"Let me go," said Elfr. "We were just tools in all of this."

"Hardly," said Bjorn. "You covered for a creature that for years fed on the most defenseless in Fensalir. Your crimes are innumerable. You have to answer for them."

"Do I?" said Elfr.

The roof of the building they were in began peeling back and standing over everyone was a troll.

"That's enough," said Bjorn.

He rushed over and tapped Elfr on the head. Elfr instantly fell to the ground, unconscious. Bjorn then jumped through the roof and landed on the troll's back. He brought his fist down on the creature's head and took it to the ground.

"Wow," said Mimir.

Liótr shook Dana to wake her up as the chaos of Skadi and the jötunn's battle raged.

"Dana. Wake up. We have to get out of here," he said as she started to stir.

"What happened?" she said.

The ground shook with every violent clash of Skadi and the Jötunn. Lightning struck the soil and water, and black clouds swirled like the early stages of a tornado or hurricane.

"Is that . . ." said Dana. "Is that Skadi?"

"They've been going at it like nothing I've ever seen," said Liótr. "I can hardly follow their movements. We must get out of here. Can you walk?"

"I think so," said Dana as Liótr assisted her to her feet.

Lightning blasted the ground directly in front of them. The force of its impact sent the two council members hurling through the air.

"Dana, are you ok?" said Liótr.

He rushed over to her and, to his dismay, found her impaled on an upturned tree branch. Blood was pouring from her wound and her mouth.

"Dana," he shouted.

"I deserve this," she said.

"I can get you out of here," said Liótr.

"It's okay."

"It's not okay. This is not how things were supposed to work out," he said.

"We made a deal with a monster, and we became monsters," she said.

"We had no choice."

"We always have a choice," she said.

"Dana, I love you," said Liótr.

"I know you do," she said.

Liótr grabbed Dana's hand and dropped his head.

Skadi and the jötunn tussled with each other, swords clashing. To Liótr, it looked like all of Midgard was shaking under the weight and explosiveness of their battle. Then, the ground split beneath him. He looked down just in time to see Midgard swallow him up.

Ridill cut the left cheek of the jötunn, and the creature grabbed its face. The wound healed, and the beast smirked.

"That is never going to work," said the jötunn. "All that time wasted going on your journey to collect the Yggdrasil roots and for what? So that you can better appreciate my power?"

"Hmph," said Skadi.

"Not so tough now," said the jötunn.

He launched into another furious attack. Skadi defended well enough, but she did have a realization. She was never going to win unless something changed and changed soon.

The jötunn let up on its attack, and Skadi caught her breath.

"You're getting tired," said the creature. "Shame. I haven't had a challenge like this in quite some time. I almost forgot what it's like to be unsure."

The jötunn stepped forward, but Skadi held her ground. The jötunn moved even closer, so it was now on top of her.

"Make a move," said the jötunn.

"Mom," shouted Bjorn.

The jötunn looked the boy's way who was dragging Elfr. Skadi took advantage of the monster's distraction and made a move for Dáinsleif, but the jötunn saw what she was doing and jumped backward.

"Not so fast," said the creature.

"Mom let me help," shouted Bjorn.

"You stay back, son. I can do this," she shouted.

"I made this journey with you, mom. We can do this together," shouted Bjorn.

"But Elfr," Skadi shouted.

"I got him," shouted Eirdóttir.

Skadi looked at the jötunn who had started walking towards her. She observed the sword that hung by his side and the powerful claws that clutched it.

The jötunn picked up speed, and right away, he was on top of her again. The two battled it out with beautiful and violent swordplay that made Midgard shake.

"I can help her, but she won't accept it," said Bjorn to Mimir. "What do I do?"

"Your mom fears for your safety, but she won't win by herself. You need to help, but if she doesn't accept your help on the battlefield, you'll be a distraction for her, and you both will lose," said Mimir.

"So, what do I do?" said Bjorn.

"You have to get at the source of her fear," said Mimir.

"The source of her fear?" whispered Bjorn.

Bjorn watched as Skadi grappled with the jötunn and kneed the creature in its abdomen multiple times before the monster stopped her and threw her into the air. He followed her skyward before briefly losing sight of her above the clouds. He could hear her deflect the jötunn's attack as he followed after her. Bjorn then saw the creature come crashing back to Midgard, where he landed with a deafening thud. Skadi touched ground shortly after, near Bjorn.

"Mom, you have to let me help you. You gave me the other half of the root. I should be as strong as you now," said Bjorn.

"It's not about strength," said Mimir.

Bjorn looked at Mimir.

"Then what is it about?"

The jötunn swiped at Skadi with Dáinsleif. She ducked, and the sword just barely missed her scalp. Skadi attempted to strike the jötunn with Ridill, but he deflected and kept her on the defensive. He toyed with her, pushing her around the battlefield. Her movements were slowing down, and it was only a matter of time until he got his one hit with the dwarven sword that didn't fail to kill its target.

"Dad's death was not your fault," shouted Bjorn. "I know that now, and I'm sorry I couldn't realize it sooner."

Skadi blocked the jötunn and jumped backward. Then, her attention shifted to her son.

"I didn't realize it until now, but you must have thought it was your fault also. Dad made his decision to help us. So let me help you," said Bjorn.

At that moment, she remembered her husband and his desire to help defend her and Bjorn from a group of attackers and her insistence that she fight alone.

"He should have let me handle it by myself," she whispered. "I can't make the same mistake again."

The jötunn took advantage of Skadi's momentary distraction and descended on her with all his power. She looked up and saw the monster dropping with his sword, prepared for what would surely be a killing blow.

Skadi put up Ridill to block, but a barrage of arrows pierced the jötunn as he fell. The beast ate the attack but diverted from his attempt on Skadi.

Skadi looked to her side after Bjorn jumped onto the battlefield by her side.

"I can help you," he said.

"Son . . ." said Skadi. "How many arrows do you have left?"

"That was it," he said.

"Then take Ridill," she said, handing him the sword. "It'll work against Dáinsleif."

"What will you use?" said Bjorn.

Skadi clenched her fists.

The jötunn pulled himself to his feet.

"I've killed over two thousand times these past few centuries. Men. Women. Children. Of all species. You are just two more souls. You're not special just because some fool has made you think you are," said the jötunn.

"No one has made us think we're special," said Skadi.

"We are doing what we have to," said Bjorn.

"As am I," said the jötunn.

Skadi led the assault, but she and her son went blow for blow with the dark creature. She had to admit to herself that they were quite the pair. They operated in sync with one another, following up hit after hit and defending, when necessary, in a coordinated fashion that left the jötunn stunned.

The lightning strikes increased, and the battlefield was now barren. The swamp crashed onto the land like ocean waves. The jötunn made for Bjorn, and Skadi tackled the creature into the dirt. The jötunn tried to strike her down with Dáinsleif, but Bjorn countered and pierced the creature through its chest. Ridill protruded from the monster's back.

Skadi positioned herself next to Bjorn as he pulled the sword free. The jötunn stepped backward and touched his chest. The wound healed.

"There's no way," said Bjorn.

"Don't you see the futility of your efforts?" said the jötunn. "If you keep doing the same thing with the same results, that makes you a fool."

"Then we need a new approach," said Skadi.

Skadi looked at her son and, with a quick gesture of her eyes, directed Bjorn's attention towards the creature's legs. Bjorn dove for the creature's legs. The jötunn stepped backward, but Bjorn shifted his body quickly, clipping the creature's legs with his own. Then, as the jötunn lost his balance, Skadi ripped Dáinsleif from the creature's hand. The Jötunn was stunned by what they'd done.

"How?" he said.

Skadi took the sword and cut the monster's head off in one clean stroke. The jötunn's eyes shot wide as its head tumbled through the dirt.

"Fool, you know that won't kill me," said the jötunn.

"Just one good hit from this sword, and you're done," said Skadi.

The jötunn looked at Dáinsleif in her hand.

"Shit," he said.

The jötunn's body fell to its knees and crashed down in the Midgardian soil.

"You're beaten," said Bjorn, and he stabbed Ridill into the monster's head through his temple.

Eirdóttir dragging Elfr and holding Mimir, ran onto the battlefield.

"Well done, you two," said Mimir. "

"You did good," said Eirdóttir.

"Where is Frija?" said Skadi.

Eirdóttir shook her head.

"She's gone, I'm afraid," said Mimir. "Before you returned, the jötunn found her and killed her."

"She isn't . . . wasn't what she said she was," said Mimir. "Frija was not a witch."

Elfr perked up.

"What was she?" he said.

"She was an Asgardian," said an ethereal voice.

Skadi first, then quickly everyone after, turned to see the ghostly image of Frija standing before them.

"I'm proud of all of you," said Frija.

"Who . . . what are you?" said Skadi.

"I am the goddess Frigg," she said.

"Frigg," said Skadi in pure astonishment. "The mother of Baldr and the wife of Odin?"

"Former wife," she said. "That love ended when he exiled me to Fensalir. In the beginning, I was pure rage, but in time I came to love the people of this town. Skadi, I saw an opportunity with you. I knew if you consumed the Yggdrasil Roots, you would have the strength to defeat this creature, but you would also have the strength to be my champion in the halls of Asgard and win me my freedom. But it seems even my plans don't always go accordingly. But I am glad you were able to kill this creature."

"I told you your plan would not go as you thought," said Mimir.

"I am bound for the afterlife. So, I need a Valkyrie to escort me," said Frija looking at Eirdóttir.

"I lost my wings," said Eirdóttir. "I am no longer a Valkyrie."

"Wings are not what make you a Valkyrie," said Frija. "Besides, did you not eat the Yggdrasil root that Skadi brought you two?"

"I did," said Eirdóttir.

"Then try spreading your wings," said Frija.

Eirdóttir did as instructed, and as if they had never been missing, her wings appeared, wider and more beautiful than ever.

"Shall we?" said Frija.

"Wait," said Skadi.

"What is it?" said Frija.

"What do we do now?" Skadi asked.

"You have the power to set your own path and be a beacon for your people. Tough times are ahead, and Midgard will need strong people to step up," said Frija. "I saw potential in you, and even now, it has not yet been fully realized. Take care of your boy."

Skadi extended her hand. Frija, though she was ghostly, formed hers around Skadi's, and the two shook.

"Lo, there do I see my father. Lo, there do I see my mother and my sisters and my brothers. Lo, there do I see the line of my people back to the beginning. Lo, do they call to me, they bid me take my place among them in the halls of Valhalla, where thine enemies have been vanquished, where the brave shall live forever. Nor shall we mourn but rejoice for those that have died the glorious death," said Skadi.

"I will be back," said Eirdóttir before taking Frija by the shoulder and disappearing together.

"So, what should we do with him?" said Mimir referring to Elfr.

"That's a good question," said Skadi.

"There's a lot of work that needs to be done. Parts of Fensalir have fallen into disrepair," said Bjorn.

"Manual labor it is. For now," said Skadi.

"Mom, the other one got away. We don't know where to find her," said Bjorn.

"Which one is that?" said Skadi.

"Lofn," said Mimir. "She can summon the dead, and it looks like two powerful council members lost their lives on that battlefield. That could be a problem down the road."

"We should get started on tracking her down as soon as possible," said Skadi.

"Agreed," said Mimir.

"Elfr, before you get to work, summon a troll to excavate the cave where the jötunn fed," said Skadi. "There are a lot of parents in this town who need closure."

TWENTY-NINE

HE LIVES

Months Later

Arey and Erik were preparing to wrap things up for the night when the door to their inn opened, and the bell at the front desk started ringing.

"Coming," said Arey.

She walked downstairs and was stunned by who she saw.

"It's you," she said.

"I'm glad you took my advice," said Skadi.

"It was starting to get a little hostile out that way," said Arey.

"Arey, who is it?" said Erik from the top of the stairs.

"The woman who saved us from those ruffians a few months ago," said Arey.

"We would like a room," Skadi said.

Arey noticed Bjorn enter the inn and stand by his mom.

"Horses are hitched," he said.

"Yes, of course," said Arey.

She grabbed a key off the wall behind her.

"Follow me," Arey said.

Skadi and Bjorn followed Arey up the stairs of the inn.

"Did you ever make it to Fensalir?" said Arey.

"We did," said Skadi. "It's our new home. We are just taking a trip."

"We wish we could have stayed where we were, but Midgard is getting absurd. So, we had to move into a town," said Arey. "We think about what you two did for us every day, though. Not a lot of people like you folks around."

Skadi smiled.

"Here is your room," said Arey and passed her the key.

"Thank you," said Skadi.

"Let me or my husband know if you need anything," said Arey.

"We will," Skadi said.

Arey nodded and let them be.

Skadi and Bjorn entered the room, and Bjorn sat his bag down on the table near the window. He unzipped it and pulled out Mimir.

"Finally," he said. "You two have fun catching up with the innkeeper?"

"Sorry, Mimir," said Bjorn.

"It's fine," he said.

"Months on the road, and we're nowhere closer to finding Lofn or my body," said Mimir.

"Do you think your body is even in Midgard? Aren't you able to see everything in the world because of Odin's ravens?" said Bjorn.

"I can only see what they are focused on, which at the time was Fensalir because of Frija's presence there. Now it's scattered. But Lofn is gone. She did not have enough time to evade those ravens before her disappearance, so she is off-world," said Mimir.

"Hmph," said Skadi.

Skadi remained by the room's door as Bjorn took a seat at the edge of the bed nearest the desk.

"You look like something is on your mind," said Mimir.

"Quiet," she said.

"What is it?" whispered Bjorn.

"We have a visitor. And I can't move," she said.

"You can't move?" said Mimir.

"I can't either," said Bjorn.

Arey opened the door of the inn, and a man walked in. Before she could say something, he put his finger to his lips and opened his pelt to show her his sword. Arey put her hands in the air and backed away from the man.

"Call your husband and get out," whispered the man.

Arey nodded.

"Erik," she said. "Please come here."

"What is it?" he said.

As soon as he arrived at the top of the steps, he saw.

"Hey . . ." said Erik.

The man put his finger to his lips.

"Just come down here," said Arey.

He did as instructed and met her at the base of the stairs.

"Get out of here," said the man.

Erik took Arey's hand, and the two exited the premises. The man looked up the stairs and began his ascent.

"Skadi. Bjorn. What do you mean you can't move?" said Mimir.

"I mean, I am stuck," said Skadi. "I cannot move at all."

"Mom, what's happening?" said Bjorn.

"I don't know, son," she replied.

The door to their room opened, and in walked the man. He wasn't immediately visible to either due to the direction they were facing. It wasn't until he spoke that they both realized who it was.

"Skadi," he said.

"I thought you were dead," she said.

"I thought I was too," said the man.

"Hovard, if this is about revenge let my son be," pleaded Skadi.

"Bjorn, I'm going to tell you something about your mother that you are not going to like," said Hovard.

"What are you talking about? How have you trapped us?" said Bjorn.

Hovard held up a rune stone for Skadi to see.

"Powerful magic enchanted this rune," said Hovard. "I know a skilled rune writer."

Skadi tried to move against Hovard, but she couldn't budge even an inch.

"Let us go," she shouted.

"Long ago, your mother belonged to my clan of Vikings. We were together for years, doing what we wanted when we wanted. We were quite the force to be reckoned with. Feared throughout the land," said Hovard.

"You were feared. We did what you wanted, not what we wanted," said Skadi.

"In my entire life, I have only loved two things," said Hovard. "The freedom of being able to roam Midgard as an untouchable and . . . my son."

"Your son was a bastard," said Skadi.

"My son was my life," shouted Hovard.

"Please just let Bjorn go," said Skadi.

"Mom," shouted Bjorn.

"One day, your father comes along. He and your mom instantly fancy each other, and it isn't long after that she is pregnant with you," said Hovard.

"Hovard stop," said Skadi.

"Get out of here," said Mimir.

"Quiet head. This does not concern you," said Hovard. "Anyway, early into your mom's pregnancy, our clan of Vikings was attacked by a rival clan."

"You're forgetting details," said Skadi.

"Am I?" shouted Hovard. "We were attacked in the middle of the night. Our men and women were being slaughtered. My son, along with your mother and father, began to fight back. I saw them fighting side by side, but I was cut off and couldn't get to them."

"Hovard," said Skadi.

"Shut it," he shouted.

"Bjorn, your mother and father wanted to leave our clan. It was your father's idea. He always wanted to raise you in Fensalir. But being a Viking meant committing yourself to your clan, to your family. But when we were attacked, your father and your mother saw an opportunity. The only thing in their way was my son," said Hovard. "Skadi's cousin."

"Your son invited that attack on us."

"When the battle was nearing its conclusion, and we had almost fought off our attackers, your father and mother stabbed my son in the back," said Hovard.

"You're lying," said Skadi.

"I saw the whole thing. He was the most adamant about you two staying with the clan. He was your biggest obstacle to leaving. I know this. And when an opportunity arose to be rid of him, you took it," said Hovard.

"That's not at all how it happened. Your son provoked the attack the day before by killing your rival's daughter when she would not wed him. Then when they attacked, he was going to kill your rival's youngest child Agata. We stopped that from happening," said Skadi.

"Shut up," shouted Hovard. "You killed Magnús. You took my child from me, and now I will do the same to you."

"Hovard, please. You are mistaken," pleaded Skadi.

Hovard touched the wall of the room, and it caught fire.

Arey and Erik looked up at the window of Bjorn and Skadi's room.

"Do you see flames?" said Erik.

"What is happening?"

"I don't know."

"We have to do something," said Arey.

Hovard walked over to Bjorn. He held out his hand and touched the boy's face.

"I hold his life in my hands like you held my boy's," said Hovard. "Skadi, do you have anything you want to say to him? This is more than you offered me."

"I will kill you," she shouted. "Don't hurt him."

"Mom," shouted Bjorn as Hovard's hand grew hotter.

"There is no pain like the loss of a child," said Hovard.

"Hovard, stop this madness," shouted Mimir.

A tear formed in Bjorn's eyes as Hovard started to burn his skin. The entire room was on fire, and smoke was clouding the ceiling.

Then a sword took Hovard's hand. It fell to the ground and rolled under the bed on which Bjorn was sitting.

"We kept one of the swords," said Arey.

In his confusion, Hovard didn't notice Erik steal the rune from his other hand. Bjorn and Skadi were free. They leaped to subdue Hovard and Skadi knocked him unconscious.

"Thank you," she said to Arey and Erik.

"We owed a debt," said Arey.

The group gathered outside of the inn with Hovard at their feet.

"That was close," said Bjorn.

"Too close," Mimir said.

Hovard peeked one eye open. He cauterized the wound and blasted off.

"Hey," shouted Bjorn.

He jumped after him but just barely missed him.

"He won't stop," said Mimir. "What do we do when he shows up again?"

"We'll think of something. We'll have to," said Skadi.

"Looks like we are officially out of the inn business now," said Arey as the building burst into raging flames.

"I'm sorry about this," said Skadi.

"Don't you two worry," Mimir said. "I know some dwarves with gold to spare. But first, we'll need to recharge the Bifrost key."

EPILOGUE

"You don't get to take a break until I say so," said Eirdóttir to Elfr.

"If I could just use one troll . . ."

"No. You have used others for far too long. Now you have to do it yourself."

"But this could be so much faster . . ."

"It's not about speed. It's about justice."

Elfr grumbled, then swung his ax again into the side of the nearest pine.

"I take it you're in charge here?" said a man who approached from behind her.

She turned around, startled by the sudden appearance of a man unfamiliar to her.

"Who are you?" she said.

"I'm looking for the person who killed my father, Farbauti."

"Who?" said Eirdóttir.

"Farbauti. He was the jötunn who lived in Fensalir. He was murdered not too long ago."

"The jötunn was your dad?" said Eirdóttir, instantly going for her sword.

"You'll have no need for that. I've come just to talk," said the man with his hands raised.

"And who are you?" said Eirdóttir.

"The name . . . is Loki."

ABOUT THE AUTHOR

Steven Williams is an avid traveler, amateur cook, and fantasy author. He is a graduate of Northwestern University and lives in Harrisburg, Pennsylvania with his wife Danielle. Skadi is his debut novel.

www.ingramcontent.com/pod-product-compliance
Lightning Source LLC
Chambersburg PA
CBHW030517020726
47494CB00004B/1135